The lights in Andi's house went out, leaving only the glow of the fire.

Bryce reached for Andi, tension spiking through him. "Stay here."

He pulled his flashlight from his pocket and clicked it on. There were no storms in the area. He'd stepped from his car under a clear sky, an almost half-moon casting its soft glow over the landscape. No reason for the power to go out.

"What happened?" Andi's voice was paper-thin, with an underlying quiver.

"I'm going to look out and see if there's light in my direction."

Bryce darted down the hall to the master bedroom. When he swept aside the curtains, his uneasiness ratcheted up several notches. A soft glow shone through the trees: his own porch light. His power was on.

So what happened to Andi's?

Out front, glass shattered, followed by an almost simultaneous scream. He dropped the curtains into place and ran from the room, panic pounding at his heels. At the end of the hall, flames engulfed the love seat that separated the living room from the dining area.

Carol J. Post writes fun and fast-paced inspirational romantic suspense stories and lives in sunshiny central Florida. She sings and plays the piano for her church and also enjoys sailing, hiking and camping—almost anything outdoors. Her daughters and grandkids live too far away for her liking, so she now pours all that nurturing into taking care of two fat and sassy cats and one highly spoiled dachshund.

Books by Carol J. Post

Love Inspired Suspense

Midnight Shadows
Motive for Murder
Out for Justice
Shattered Haven
Hidden Identity
Mistletoe Justice
Buried Memories
Reunited by Danger
Fatal Recall
Lethal Legacy

LETHAL LEGACY

CAROL J. POST

◆ HARLEQUIN® LOVE INSPIRED® SUSPENSE

Recycling programs for this product may not exist in your area.

LOVE INSPIRED BOOKS

ISBN-13: 978-1-335-49061-2

Lethal Legacy

www.Harlequin.com

Printed in U.S.A.

Fear thou not; for I am with thee: be not dismayed;
for I am thy God: I will strengthen thee;
yea, I will help thee; yea, I will uphold thee
with the right hand of my righteousness.
—Isaiah 41:10

Writing is a solitary activity,
but a lot of support goes into writing
and publishing a book. A huge thank-you to my "team":

My sister, Kim Wolff,
for all your help with my Murphy research.

The rest of my family for your unending encouragement.

My critique partners, Karen Fleming and Sabrina Jarema,
for making my stories the best they can be.

My beta reader/proofreader, Martha "Mom" Post,
for catching the things the rest of us miss.

My amazing editor, Dina Davis,
and lovely agent, Nalini Akolekar, for all your hard work.

And my wonderful husband, Chris,
for thirty-seven amazing years.

ONE

Trees lined both sides of the gravel drive. Their half-bare limbs framed the old house at its end and lent a spooky edge to the air of abandonment that hung over the property. A branch dangled from an oak, curled leaves barely visible against the moonlit sky.

Andrea Wheaton slowed her Escalade to a crawl. It didn't help. The long screech against the roof set her teeth on edge and sent a shiver down her spine.

At the end of the drive, she released a sigh as childhood memories bombarded her. The old Wheaton place projected a rustic hominess that had always called to her. It didn't hold a candle to their place in Atlanta, with its soaring columns and manicured grounds, but she'd always loved it. It had represented freedom, the one place she could let down her guard and simply be Andi.

Now it was hers. Six days later, and she was still reeling from the news.

She retrieved her small suitcase from the back seat and carried it to a porch covered with a three-inch-deep blanket of dead leaves. A swing hung from one end, and two Adirondack rockers sat side by side in the center. Judging from the layer of debris on each, neither the swing nor the rockers had been used for some time.

She laid the bag down and then pulled a wooden key chain from her purse. It was cut into the shape of North Carolina, the word *Murphy* burned onto its face. For twelve years, the key had lain in the bottom of her jewelry box, untouched. Partly because she'd been busy, first with college, and then with marriage and job responsibilities. Partly because she'd wanted to avoid the neighbors on both sides.

One she'd never cared for. The other she'd cared for too much.

When she slid the key into the lock, it turned without resistance. She frowned. Had her father forgotten to lock the dead bolt? A quick check of the doorknob told her it was unlocked, too.

A wave of uneasiness swept over her, and she shook it off. This wasn't the city. This was Murphy, North Carolina, where neighbors helped one another out and it wasn't uncommon to see a car parked in front of the Daily Grind downtown, keys still in the ignition.

She opened the door and swiped the double switch inside. Light flooded the porch and living room. When she stepped over the threshold, a sense of grief cut a wide swath through her heart. This had been her and her father's retreat, the opportunity for them to escape the incessant demands of her mother.

Less than a week ago, she'd been sitting at the huge table in her aunt and uncle's lodge near Asheville, enjoying turkey dinner, her parents across from her. Now they were gone. After leaving the lodge, they'd apparently taken a curve too fast and plunged down an embankment to their deaths. Driving fast wasn't in her dad's nature. Neither was carelessness.

But neither was moodiness. Or brooding. Or several other behaviors she'd seen over the past months. Lately, her fun-loving father had become someone else entirely.

Something had been bothering him. Now she'd never know what.

After locking the door, she lowered her carry-on and extended the handle. The wheels rumbled against the hardwood floor as she made her way to the first bedroom. It had always been hers. When her grandparents were alive, the second one had been her dad's. He'd long since taken the master bedroom and reallocated the middle one as an office.

She laid the bag on her bed and transferred the contents to the chest of drawers. She hadn't brought much. The purpose of the trip was to scout out the place, see how much it had deteriorated over the past twelve years and decide what to do with it.

The decision about the Atlanta place was a no-brainer. As marketing director for a large sporting goods manufacturer, she spent more hours at work than at home. Her two-bedroom condo was plenty of house for her. She'd already contacted a Realtor, and her parents' seven-thousand-square-foot spread was going on the market next week.

This one was harder to let go. It had been in her dad's family for three generations. Four, if she counted her own.

After shutting the last drawer, she picked up her toiletry case and headed for the bathroom. As she stepped into the hall, something moved in her peripheral vision. She snapped her gaze in that direction.

A huge man barreled toward her. Except for two eye-holes, a knit mask hid his face. He slammed into her, knocking her hard against the wall. Her head hit the doorjamb. Pain shot through her temple and stars exploded across her vision.

Another figure ran past, this one much smaller. As retreating footsteps grew softer, blackness encroached. She gripped the jamb, willing herself to remain conscious, but strength drained from her limbs. She slid to the floor, landing on her hands and knees.

The front door creaked open but didn't slam shut. They'd left it ajar. She needed to secure the house. And she needed to call the police. The front door seemed miles away. The bedroom was just across the hall, and her purse was on the bed. If she could crawl there…

She moved her right knee forward, followed by her right hand. The darkness spread, seeping in from all sides. The walls tipped ninety degrees, and the cold floor met her right side.

She lifted one lead-filled arm, trying to grasp the last threads of consciousness.

Her hand fell.

And even that small circle of light faded and disappeared.

Bryce Caldwell flipped on the cruiser's right signal and made his turn onto Ranger Road. As he accelerated up the steep incline, his headlights spilled over the tombstones dotting the landscape. The street cut right through Ranger United Methodist's cemetery.

He rounded a series of curves, following Ranger as it snaked its way upward. His gaze shifted left, the same as it always did. Since night had fallen some time ago, there was nothing to see. But that didn't stop him from looking. He'd been doing it as long as he could remember.

Many years ago, his reasons had been romantic. Now they were entirely practical. His neighbor spent most of his time in Atlanta and had asked him to keep an eye on the place.

Bryce tapped the brakes. Lights were on at the old house, and a vehicle was parked out front. There wasn't enough light to identify the make, but it was too large to be Dennis Wheaton's Mercedes.

He pulled into his own driveway a couple hundred yards down. As he approached his house, a black face nudged aside the vertical blinds hanging at the living room window. Cooper greeted him with a single bark. The dog would have to wait a few minutes longer. Since lights were on next door, the visitor was likely there with Wheaton's knowledge and permission. But it would take only a few minutes to check.

He turned around and retraced his route. As he crept up the drive next door, his jaw tightened. The front door was wide-open, and no one was outside. He stopped behind the vehicle, a newer Cadillac Escalade, and stepped from the cruiser.

"Hello?"

Silence met his call. He moved past the SUV, and a chilly gust swept through, sending the leaves at his feet into a frantic dance. When he stepped onto the porch, he called again. Still silence. Who would leave the front door open and not be somewhere nearby?

"Hello?" Now he was at the doorway, half in and half out. "Anybody home?"

A moan came from the hallway. His senses shot to full alert, and he drew his weapon. When he stepped into the hall, a woman was working her way onto her hands and knees. Strawberry blond hair had fallen forward to hide her face.

He rushed toward her, still scanning the area. He wasn't about to let down his guard.

"Are you alone?"

She lifted her head. Blue eyes met his, sending a jolt all the way to his toes. *Andi.* Years fell away, each one a punch to his gut. She'd left just before he started college, after he'd made the biggest mistake of his life. And she'd managed to stay away for twelve long years.

Her gaze slid from his face, down his uniform and back up again. Instead of recognition, her eyes held confusion. "Did I call? I didn't think I…" She sat back, one leg curled beneath her, the other in front. "I tried, but…" She fell silent, shaking her head.

He knelt in front of her. "Tell me what happened."

"Someone was inside, knocked me into the doorjamb." She pressed a palm to her left temple. "I hit my head."

Her assailant must have run out the front, leaving the door wide-open. Bryce slid his pistol back into its holster. "He's probably gone, but we need to call it in."

The furrows between her brows deepened. "Who are you?"

Bryce Caldwell. It was right on the tip of his tongue. But considering how they'd parted, he'd better save specifics for later. "I'm with Cherokee County, but I'm not on duty. I just happened to be driving by. We'll get this reported officially. Then you need to go to the hospital and get checked out."

"I'm fine." She gripped the bedroom doorjamb and pulled herself to her feet. Even holding on, she swayed.

If she thought standing would convince him she didn't need medical attention, she was sadly mistaken.

"You probably have a concussion. You need to be seen."

She shook her head. "I've got too much to do to spend several hours in a hospital emergency room."

He frowned. If she let go of that wall, she'd be flat on her face. But it was no use arguing. She'd developed a stubborn streak that hadn't been there before.

"Let me at least get you to the couch. You need to sit before you fall down."

When she took the hand he offered, he led her into the living room, where the sofa, love seat and recliner formed a U-shape around a stone fireplace. He and Andi had spent countless winter weekends sitting on that hearth, roasting s'mores.

After he'd seated her on the love seat, he pulled out his phone. One bar. He wasn't surprised. He always lost service at the bridge shortly before turning onto Ranger, and then didn't pick it up again until somewhere between the Wheaton property and his own.

Without touching the open door, he stepped onto the porch for a clearer signal. When he introduced himself to the dispatcher, he smiled at the sharp intake of air behind him.

He wasn't surprised she didn't recognize him. Even if she hadn't conked her head, it wouldn't have been easy. Through his teen years, he'd been tall and lanky and had worn his hair on the long side. Now it could almost be classified as a buzz cut. Though he was still six-two, he'd packed on fifty pounds of muscle since his teenage years.

Once finished with dispatch, he sat on the couch opposite her. "Do you know who accosted you?"

"No. They were both wearing ski masks."

"Both?"

"After the larger guy hit me, another one ran out behind him."

He nodded. The confusion she'd displayed earlier had left, and stiffness had settled in, leaving the air thick with tension. Maybe she'd stay long enough for him to try to rebuild some bridges. Probably not. He didn't even know why she'd come. But it wasn't important. There were more pressing matters.

Bryce glanced around the room. "Any idea what they were after?"

Nothing appeared disturbed. Of course, the house had never held the usual items that attracted thieves. Other than a telescope that had been top-of-the-line twenty years ago, there wasn't any equipment, electronic or otherwise. As far as he knew, the Wheatons had never had TVs or computers.

That wasn't why they came to Murphy. Weekends here were for family time, outdoor activities, hanging with friends. Usually it was just Andi and her dad. Bryce had met Andi's mother twice and hadn't been impressed either time. She'd seemed cold and hard. And quite haughty.

Fortunately, Andi took after her father.

She shrugged. "Probably the usual things. Cash, jewelry, anything that can be pawned quickly. Empty houses make easy targets."

She pushed herself to her feet. When he hurried to help her, she waved away his hand. She seemed steadier than when she'd let him lead her into the room. She also knew who he was.

She moved away from him, arms extended for balance. "I think I walked in on them before they got very far. Nothing's disturbed here or in my room. I haven't checked the others."

He followed her down the hall. "Your dad didn't come with you?"

The glance she cast over her shoulder was brief, but the pain on her face shot straight to his heart.

"My dad—"

Her words ended in a gasp. She'd stopped at an open doorway and stood staring into the room, mouth agape.

"What is it?" He rushed up next to her and stifled his own gasp.

It was Dennis Wheaton's office. Someone had trashed it.

Every book had been pulled from the shelves. The empty bookcase lay on top. Desk drawers added to the mess, their contents strewn about, the drawers themselves upside down on the mound. The telescope that had occupied the corner of the room lay on its side. The closet had been ransacked, too. Years' worth of Christmas decorations lay in a heap, the empty boxes tossed aside.

Andi slumped against the doorjamb, and he resisted the urge to pull her into his arms. Twelve years ago, she'd have appreciated it. Not now.

"This was uncalled for." She swept one arm toward the mess. "They obviously weren't happy to find nothing more valuable than an old telescope."

Bryce frowned. She was probably right. What house in the twenty-first century didn't have an array of televisions, laptops, iPads and game consoles?

He looked around the office and shook his head. *Hobby room* would have been a more appropriate name. The space had never held Dennis's accounting, financial-planning or business books. Instead, the items that littered the floor bore titles such as *Astronomy 101*, *The Elegant Universe* and *Earth, Space and Beyond*, along with numerous art-related books.

Art had been Andi's passion, astronomy all of theirs. Many nights, her dad had set up the telescope on the back deck, and the three of them had studied the sky. Stargazing had been one of many activities he'd shared with Dennis Wheaton. Andi's dad was the father he'd never had.

Well, he *had* a father. Bryce just hadn't seen him often enough for it to count. On those rare occasions when the old man *did* pop in, the visits had done more harm than good. If it weren't for Dennis Wheaton's influence, Bryce's life would have taken a different turn.

"I need to call your dad."

She looked at him, eyes glistening with unshed tears. "You can't. He was killed in a car accident on Thanksgiving Day."

His breath whooshed out and he slumped against the wall. A sense of emptiness swept through him, as cold and dark as space itself. "How?"

"I don't know. He missed a curve and drove off a cliff."

Bryce slid down the wall until he came to a seated position against it. Dennis Wheaton was gone. He couldn't be. This had to be a bad dream.

But it *was* real, just like the woman standing in front of him, looking as broken as he felt.

He shook his head. "That's why he didn't come."

"What?"

Sirens sounded in the distance. The police would be

there shortly. He crossed his arms, trying to stave off a sudden chill.

"Your dad was here the Tuesday night before Thanksgiving. The next day, he called and said he wanted to meet with me that weekend. When he didn't show up, I figured he'd gotten busy."

Andi righted the desk chair and lowered herself into it. "Did he say why he wanted to meet?"

"Just that he wanted to talk with me. He sounded like a man ready to unload a heavy burden. I asked him if everything was okay. He said, 'It will be soon.'"

Her eyebrows lifted and her jaw dropped as the color drained from her face.

"Andi?" He rose to put a hand on her shoulder.

"Living with my mother wasn't easy, but he always seemed to not let her criticism bother him. For the past few months, though, things were different."

"Different how?"

"Something had been weighing him down. He seemed preoccupied, even depressed. I tried to talk to him, but he kept denying anything was wrong." She crossed her arms over her stomach. "The signs were there, and I didn't recognize them."

"What signs? What are you talking about?"

"Depression, withdrawal. Losing interest in activities he'd always enjoyed, like coming up here." She lifted her head, and her gaze locked with his. "The comment he made to you—that everything was going to be okay soon. It's all clear now. I should have seen it."

Now he knew where her thoughts had gone. And how much sense they made. Maybe Dennis had called him to talk about his struggles, guy-to-guy, not wanting to unload on Andi, then hadn't been able to hold out any longer. Or maybe he'd gotten involved in something he regretted and wanted to clear his conscience but hadn't had what it took to face the consequences.

No, not Dennis. He had too much integrity. And he loved life too much.

Andi's brows drew together, and her eyes filled with pain. "When I add it all together, I'm afraid my dad drove off that mountain intentionally. And he took my mother with him."

TWO

Andrea tipped back her head and stared into the endless expanse. Stars were strewn across the sky from horizon to horizon, like rhinestones against black velvet. She tightened her hands around the steaming mug of herbal tea, soaking in the heat.

She'd gotten enough accomplished today to feel good about sitting on the back deck and doing nothing. She'd given the place a deep cleaning and put everything back in its proper place. Then she'd made a list of repairs to be done, whether she sold the house or kept it. Most important, she'd had a handyman replace the broken pane in the living room window. It was how the assailants had gained access. Though the missing piece of glass was obvious in the daylight, she hadn't noticed it last night.

She'd hoped her cleaning would uncover some clue about what had been going on in her dad's life. The only thing she'd found raised more questions than it answered. It was a simple two-line poem, scrawled on a sheet of yellow paper torn from a legal pad—"When a secret is too heavy to keep, it's always best to bury it deep."

What was that supposed to mean? Was the secret what

he'd wanted to talk to Bryce about? Was the weight of what he'd carried so heavy he'd felt he had no way out?

She sipped the tea, relishing the heat as it traveled down her throat. The temperature had dipped as soon as the sun went down. But there was something soothing about sitting under the stars, holding the hot cup, with peaceful silence all around her.

There was a party going on right next door. Bryce and his two best friends had had a cookout and were now watching a movie. He'd invited her, even assured her she wouldn't be the only woman. One of his friends was married, the other engaged. She'd passed.

When he'd told the dispatcher his name last night, she'd almost fallen off the couch. She'd known if she spent much time at the Murphy place, she'd eventually run into him. But she hadn't thought it would be so soon. And she hadn't planned to greet him in a fog, on her hands and knees.

And she hadn't expected him to look like he did, all buff and mature. Though common sense told her he would've changed, she'd somehow held on to the image of the smiling teenager she'd fallen in love with at age fourteen.

Last night, he hadn't been smiling. And he wasn't a teenager anymore. He'd radiated confidence, maturity and a sense of power that was mesmerizing, standing above her, a pistol at his hip.

What was it about a man in uniform that women found so irresistible? Whatever it was, Bryce definitely did the Cherokee County garb justice.

Andrea swallowed the last of her tea and held the empty cup, drawing the heat from the porcelain. A wind gust swept along the back of the house, and a shiver shook her shoulders.

She stood to go back inside, then hesitated. Had she seen a glow deep in her woods? She waited for several more moments.

There, near the left-hand edge of her property. Or maybe it was coming from the Langman place and wasn't even in her woods.

The glow moved rightward in an erratic path, as if someone was walking with a flashlight. Whoever was prowling the woods was definitely on her property now. Was it the men who'd been in the house last night, coming back to finish their search?

She pulled her phone from her rear pocket and stared at the screen. If she called the police, it would take a unit twenty minutes to arrive. If the prowler was still there, he'd take off as soon as he heard sirens.

There was another option. Bryce had said to call if she needed anything. He was right next door. And he was law enforcement. Based on what he'd told her, so was one of his friends. They could be there in less than a minute, both armed.

She went back in to retrieve the business card Bryce had left on the rolltop desk and punched the number into her phone. The decision was a no-brainer. Looked like she was going to meet Bryce's friend after all. If she had cell service.

Though the phone showed one bar, the call wouldn't connect. She returned to the deck and squinted into the woods. The light was still there. When she checked the phone, the screen showed "dialing."

"Come on, connect already."

She moved across the back of the house toward

Lethal Legacy

Bryce's property. If the signal didn't get strong enough soon, she might as well go knock on his door.

She'd just reached the corner of her house when she heard the first ring. Bryce answered two rings later. There was no background noise on his end of the line. He'd either paused the movie or left the room. She told him the reason for her call. His next words were obviously not for her.

"Grab your weapon. The neighbor I told you about has another prowler."

The neighbor I told you about? What did he tell them?

Probably that someone had broken into the house next door. Even if he'd said more, what did it matter? Tomorrow she was heading back to Atlanta to be ready for Saturday's funeral. She had no intention of hanging out with Bryce and his friends, even if she kept the place and used it as an occasional retreat.

She disconnected the call, then made her way to the back door. She'd stay locked inside until Bryce and his friend arrived.

When she swung the screen door open, the outer edge dropped a half inch. The hinges needed longer screws. Something else that would have to be done.

The property wasn't in total disrepair, but since her dad had inherited the place, he'd done the bare minimum to keep it from crumbling to the ground. That was easier than listening to her mother carry on about how he was spending their hard-earned money on something he should have unloaded long ago.

Andrea frowned. *Their* hard-earned money was a misnomer, since her mother hadn't done the actual earning. With a father who was a senior partner in a huge personal-injury law firm, Margaret Cunningham-Wheaton had grown up spending money without having to worry about where it came from. And her family had made sure she could continue the habit. Going to college and falling in love with an accounting major hadn't been in anybody's plans.

Andrea paced the floor while she waited. Her one-minute estimate was overly optimistic. One minute stretched into two, then three and eventually ten. What were they doing, waiting till the movie was over?

When someone finally knocked on the back door, she flipped the exterior light on and looked out the dining room window. Instead of two men on her deck, three were lined up side by side. She swung open the door.

Bryce and a man she didn't know kept a tight grip on the one in the center. Although she hadn't recognized Bryce, Matt Langman, her other neighbor, was easily identifiable.

His face had aged, more than it should have in the past twelve years. He'd lived a rough life. According to her father, he spent half his time in jail and the other half hatching up new ways to get into trouble. There was likely plenty of drug use involved, too.

But a lot hadn't changed. He still wore his hair in the same shaggy style and maintained that signature air of indifference. The cockiness hadn't lessened one iota. He was too thin to be the one who'd slammed her into the doorjamb. But the accomplice could have been Matt. Their sizes were similar.

"What are you doing on my property?"

"Being held against my will by your boyfriend and his goon." His eyes narrowed in the same malicious glare he'd always given her.

She crossed her arms. She'd never done anything to

him, had hardly spoken to him over the years. But he'd always hated her. He despised her for her privileged up-bringing and the fact that Bryce's relationship with her and her father had ended his friendship with Matt.

But the bad blood went back further than that. Three generations, actually. Their great-grandfathers had been in business together and ended up with some irresolvable differences. Her great-grandfather had bought Matt's out at a price the Wheaton clan insisted was generous and the Langman clan swore was highway robbery. The Langmans were still holding a grudge.

"What *were* you doing on my property?"

He tried to jerk away, but Bryce and his friend tightened their hold. "Going for a walk."

"At nine thirty at night?"

He lifted his chin. "Cherokee County doesn't have a curfew."

"Doesn't matter. You're trespassing."

"Not if there aren't any signs."

Maybe he had her there. Before heading back to Atlanta, she'd stop by Tractor Supply and pick up a couple, along with a handheld staple gun. "I'll have that remedied tomorrow." Whatever Matt's reasons, he was up to no good. "In the meantime, I'm giving you verbal warning. Stay off my property, or I'll have you arrested."

"It's not yours. It's your dad's."

"Since my dad's dead, it's mine."

For a brief moment, the cockiness fell away and his eyes widened. "Are you going to live here?"

"I haven't decided what I'm doing with the place yet."

His lips curled back in a sneer. "You need to take that snooty car of yours and go back to your fancy place in Atlanta. You don't belong here."

Fire sparked inside and spread. Before she could formulate a response, Bryce gave him a shake.

"That's not for you to decide. You heard what Andi said. If you step foot on this property again, I'll arrest you myself."

Matt opened his mouth but then apparently thought better of it. Instead, he shook off the hands that held him and sauntered toward the trees separating their two properties.

Before leaving the circle of light emanating from the deck, he cast a glance over his shoulder. Even with the shadows, the hatred Andrea saw there sent a chill down her spine.

When listing the pros and cons of keeping the property, Matt definitely belonged on the con side. She wasn't about to let him push her around. But having to deal with an antagonistic neighbor needed to be a consideration in her decision. Especially when her safety was at stake.

As for Bryce, she hadn't decided whether his presence was a pro or a con.

"Stay."

Bryce extended his arm, palm angled toward Cooper. "You can't go with me this time."

He moved down the porch steps, leaving behind a pouting dog, then headed across the yard under a steel-gray sky. A cold front was moving their direction. It probably wouldn't bring snow. Murphy saw snow only a handful of times each year. November was a little early.

Today Andrea was returning to Atlanta. She'd finished the funeral arrangements before coming to Murphy but still had a lot of paperwork to get through in the Wheatons' Atlanta house.

Tomorrow he'd make the two-hour drive himself. No way was he going to pass up the opportunity to pay his final respects to the man who'd made more difference in his life than anyone else on the planet.

He stepped onto the trail that separated his property from Andi's. He'd see if Andi needed help with anything before she headed out. After the funeral tomorrow, he had no idea when he'd see her again. If ever.

Disappointment settled over him. Two days hadn't been enough time to iron out everything that was wrong between them. He wasn't sure what changes he'd expected in so short a time, but they hadn't happened.

When he reached her yard, movement drew his attention to the right. He looked that way as Andi disappeared into the woods. Where was she going?

He jogged along the side of her house and to the back. The small yard sloped down toward woods that stretched all the way to a creek at the rear edge of the ten acres. Ahead, patches of red flashed between almost bare trees. He followed, now knowing her destination.

When he reached her, she stood outside a small circular stone wall. Four posts held up a weathered roof. The crank that had at one time wound the rope to raise the bucket had frozen up years ago. He'd been there with her before. Many times.

She glanced over one shoulder before turning back to stare into the dark depths. "This was one of his favorite places." Her tone held wistfulness. "He used to say that most wells collect wishes, but this one collects burdens. Anytime something was bothering me, we would pretend to ball it up and throw it into the well."

The sadness radiating from her was almost palpable. But there was something else, too. She seemed tormented in more than a grieving sense. Her turmoil wove a path straight to his heart.

He put a hand on her shoulder, and she tensed. He dropped his arm. Would he ever be able to offer comfort as a friend and have her accept it?

"I'm sorry." So much more than two words could convey. He was sorry for the way her life had been turned upside down, sorry for the grief she felt and sorry that he'd killed any chance of a friendship with one stupid decision.

And friendship was all he hoped for. Dennis had told him about Andi's divorce, but other than a brief reference to her husband cheating on her, he hadn't given any details. All Bryce knew was she'd taken it hard. And she had walls around her heart a mile thick.

Dennis hadn't had to tell him the last part. He'd felt them for the past two days. And he didn't have what it took to break them down. A few months ago, maybe. Before he'd expended every bit of emotional energy he had on a relationship, only to have it crash and burn in the end.

A rain-scented gust whipped through, sending a shower of dried leaves down around them. Andi turned away from the well. "If I want to make my trip on dry roads, I'd better get going."

"Can I help you with anything?"

"I'm already loaded and locked up. I just wanted to come out here before I left."

He fell into step beside her. "Any idea when you'll be back?"

"Not for a while."

They crossed the small yard, then continued along the side of the house. A piece of fascia on the gable end had worked its way loose, and the wood siding needed a fresh finish. If Andi wanted to sell the place, she'd need to have some work done. Or maybe she'd keep it as a weekend getaway.

Not likely. If she'd "gotten away" anytime over the past twelve years, it hadn't been to Murphy.

He stopped in the driveway to stand next to the Escalade. "Until you decide whether to sell, I'm happy to continue keeping an eye on things. I'm sure it'll take time to settle the estate."

"Settling the estate will be the easy part." She leaned against the SUV, her brows dipping to form creases above her nose. "My dad added me to all their assets just two months ago. I didn't question it at the time. He's always been a planner. My parents have had wills as long as I can remember. But maybe this was more than good planning. Maybe he was putting his affairs in order for a reason."

She opened the driver's door and slid into the seat, shoulders hunched. "I should have asked him some questions."

"You tried. He wouldn't talk."

"He was going to talk to you."

"Then apparently changed his mind."

She nodded. "He buried it deep."

He lifted a brow.

"Last night, I picked up a book he had sitting on his nightstand. A piece of paper was sticking out of it. He'd written, 'When a secret is too heavy to keep, it's always best to bury it deep.'"

He frowned. "That secret is probably what he was going to talk to me about."

"Instead, he decided to stuff it down and hold it inside. Whatever his secret was, he took it with him when he drove off the mountain." She put the key into the ignition and cranked the engine.

He stepped back, ready to close her door. "I'll see you tomorrow."

Actually, he probably wouldn't. He'd be there, but so would half of Atlanta. He'd never been to their home church, but according to Andi, it was huge. As well connected as they'd been, it would be packed.

He'd never been crazy about big churches. Actually, he'd never been crazy about church, period. Not that he was a stranger. His mom and grandparents were what some called "Chreasters"—they attended on Christmas and Easter.

Andi's family had gone every Sunday, even while in Murphy. The church here was different from what they were used to, with a congregation of less than a hundred that met in a small building off the four-lane highway.

Bryce had usually gone with them. At that time, he'd needed it. He'd had lots of mischievousness to atone for. Now he was a law-abiding citizen, serving the people of Cherokee County. At thirty years old, his good deeds far outweighed the bad he'd done as an adolescent and young teen.

He closed Andi's door, then watched her head up the drive. If she kept the property, she'd have to visit occasionally, even with him checking on the place. It wouldn't make sense to keep up the taxes, insurance and utilities otherwise.

Of course, she could afford it. For the Wheaton family, money had never been an issue. Between her parents' wealth and what her husband made, Mrs. Wheaton had never had to work. Bryce's own mother had held a nine-to-five job in a local insurance company.

While Andi had lived in the Wheaton mansion in an exclusive Atlanta neighborhood, he and his mom had stayed with his grandparents. And during Andi's vacations to places like Switzerland, Ireland and Paris, his family had visited relatives or camped at Deep Creek.

But Andi had never let the difference in social status get in the way of their relationship. Ultimately, he had. He'd let his own insecurities push him into throwing away something special and had regretted it ever since.

He wasn't holding out unrealistic hopes of reclaiming what they'd had so long ago. There was too much water under the bridge. They were both different people now.

But if she had plans to keep the property, he hoped they could develop an amicable friendship.

Judging from her coolness toward him, maybe even that was out of reach.

The large canopy cast a shadow over those sitting beneath. Andrea occupied a chair in the front row, back straight and stiff and hands clutched in her lap. An aunt and uncle sat on either side of her. More relatives occupied the dozen or so other chairs, and numerous mourners hovered around in a loosely packed semicircle. Metal framework suspended two caskets over freshly dug graves, the pastor standing between. The sun shone from a cloudless blue sky, and nearby, squirrels chased one another up a tree.

Andrea released a sigh. The perfection of the weather mocked her own dark mood. The sad, angry skies she'd driven home under yesterday would have been more appropriate.

The pastor finished reading the twenty-third Psalm, and Andrea's uncle squeezed her shoulder. He'd kept his arm over the back of her chair, offering silent gestures of comfort. She appreciated it but didn't need it. She'd managed to sit stoically throughout the entire funeral and graveside service. She'd do her grieving in private.

After a final prayer, Andrea stood, pulling her coat more tightly around her. Yesterday's rain had brought colder temperatures, and she was having difficulty shaking the chill. As she stepped into the sunshine, a man in a suit made his way through the crowd toward her. His hairline had receded, and the salt had overtaken the pepper, but other than that, he looked the same as he had twelve years ago. He'd pastored the church all through her teenage years.

"Pastor Pierce." She shook his hand, a wave of guilt passing through her. Did he know she hadn't darkened the door of a church since she left for college?

It wasn't that she had anything against attending. Her mother had always stressed the importance of regularly attending church. But it had to be the right kind of church—large, impressive, full of quality people. It was good for the image, she'd said. With the advice always came the admonition to not get carried away with the emotionalism that went on in some of the smaller country churches, where people were poor and uneducated. Large or small, it hadn't mattered to Andrea. Since reaching adulthood, too many other things in her life had qualified as important.

She offered him a weak smile. "Thank you for coming."

"Of course." He wrapped her hand in both of his. "You and your family are in my prayers. May the Lord comfort you during this difficult time."

After accepting dozens more handshakes and hugs, Andrea made her way to one of the two limos that had transported her and the other immediate family members from the church to the cemetery. She'd take the ride back to the church and attend the dinner the hospitality committee had prepared for the family and close friends. Then she'd get to be alone. She'd survived the past nine days. She could get through the next two hours.

Her aunt Louise reached her as the limo driver opened the door. Andrea paused for the hug she knew her aunt needed. When finished, her aunt shook her head.

"I still can't believe they're gone." Fresh tears gathered on her lower lashes. "When we watched your mom get behind the wheel in our driveway, we never imagined that would be the last time we'd see either of them alive."

"My mom was driving?" There had to be a mistake. Her mom never drove if her dad was with her.

"After you left, Dennis started feeling ill. Although the offer seemed a little begrudging, your mom said she'd drive them home. Margaret has never been crazy about driving." She pursed her lips. "I can't help but think that if your dad had been the one behind the wheel, we wouldn't be here today."

Andrea sank into the seat, her feet still planted outside the car. Her mind spun, leaving her feeling light-headed.

Her father hadn't been driving. Her mother had. Whatever had been weighing on her father's mind for the past several months, he hadn't decided to take his own life.

Her aunt climbed into the car, unaware of the bombshell she'd just dropped. The news eliminated the possibility of suicide but raised a whole slew of unanswered questions. If Andrea's dad was unlikely to take a curve too fast, her mom was even more so. They'd always ribbed her about being a turtle.

Besides, the area was familiar to both of them. They were a mile from the lodge, on a winding road they'd traveled dozens of times. The brakes had to have failed. Monday, she was going to ask to have the car checked, if that wasn't already part of the investigation.

For the next hour, Andrea engaged in polite conversation and forced down food she had no desire to eat. After a socially acceptable amount of time, she said her farewells, climbed into the Escalade and pulled out of the parking lot. Since leaving home that morning, she'd looked forward to the end of the day's activities, when she could again be alone with her grief.

But now that she was headed there, home was the last place she wanted to be. Maybe she should do some more sorting at her parents' house. Keeping busy would be good for her. Throwing herself into activity had always been her default.

She cruised through an intersection on a yellow light and swiveled her head to the right. A few blocks down was a café, one of those cute places decorated with flowers and lace that served lunch on antique china. Her mom loved it.

Andrea hated it.

Nothing against the café. It was lunches with her mom in general. No matter how they started out, eventually they evolved into battles, with Andrea on the losing side every time. Her mom was the queen of unwanted advice, usually given in the form of some pithy proverb. She was also the queen of criticism.

Andrea drew in a constricted breath. As a child, she'd gone to desperate lengths to please her mother. As a teenager, she'd clung to every word of praise from her father while still trying to gain her mother's approval. As an adult, she'd given up.

She flipped on her signal and got into the left-turn lane. As her route took her within a block of Neurology and Neurosurgical Associates, the familiar tightness returned. At two o'clock in the afternoon, her ex was either there or at the hospital.

Or home enjoying her replacement.

Her divorce had been another sore spot between her and her mother. While Andrea had been reeling with betrayal, her mother's focus had been on how it was going to affect her relationship with her friends, since the Morrisons were one of the elite families of Atlanta and Phil's mother was one of her closest friends. She'd insisted that Andrea should have tried harder.

Maybe she should have. If she hadn't been so focused on climbing the corporate ladder, maybe she'd have noticed the warning signs in time to save her marriage.

Then she'd have fallen short of her mother's expectations some other way. Her dreams of mending that relationship had never materialized. Now it was too late.

She slammed her hand against the steering wheel, palm open. She'd expected the agonizing grief over losing her father. He'd been the center of her world her entire life.

What she *hadn't* expected was the guilt she felt over the poor relationship she'd always had with her mother. No matter what distractions she'd attempted, she hadn't been able to run from it.

Maybe activity wasn't what she needed. Maybe she needed the opposite. Time to decompress and let the frayed edges of her heart begin to heal.

She knew the perfect place to do it.

Everything in Atlanta reminded her of her mother or her ex, but Murphy connected her with her father. By tonight, she could be there, tucked away in the house that had been her refuge since she was old enough to appreciate the need for escape.

She was supposed to return to work on Monday. But she still had another six weeks of vacation time banked. She frowned. That in itself was a pretty good commentary on her life.

She hit the brakes and headed toward downtown. If she was going to be gone for an indefinite amount of time, she had some work to do. After being out a week and a half, her desk would be a mess. But she'd get everything whipped into shape by the end of the day, and any loose ends she couldn't tie up, she'd deal with remotely.

When she stepped from the building hours later, it was dusk. She laid her laptop case on the passenger seat. She'd use public internet until she decided whether to have it installed at the house.

For the next few weeks, she'd be right next door to Bryce. But she'd deal with that, too. She was a mature adult, not a love-struck teenager. Back then, Bryce had promised to love her with a love as big as the sky, always and forever. And she'd believed it. At the time, the words were cheesy. In hindsight, they were meaningless. In the intervening years, she'd learned there was no such thing as *always and forever*.

Thirty minutes after arriving home, she was ready to hit the road. She did enough traveling on business to know how to pack quickly. She tossed the two small bags into the back seat of the Escalade.

As she drove north on 75, then took the 575 ramp, the

weight that had been pressing down on her lifted. Taking additional time off had been a good idea. So had getting out of Atlanta. She wasn't running away; she was just... Okay, maybe she *was*.

But it was about time. She'd never run from anything. She was always forging ahead, accepting the next challenge, whether in school or work or life in general. Now she was just tired.

She made the left turn onto 60 and arched her back, working out some of the stiffness. It was the final leg of her trip. Mineral Bluff was a short distance ahead. Then she'd make her right onto Spur 60, which would take her across the state line. Ten minutes after that, she'd be lugging her bags inside and preparing for what she hoped would be a good night's sleep.

As she tapped the brakes for the first curve, headlights shone in her rearview mirror. The vehicle drew closer, and she squinted, waiting for the driver to dim his lights. He didn't. Soon he was on her tail. She rounded the curve and accelerated. The other driver did the same, maintaining a distance of one car length. Judging from the height of the headlights and distance between them, the other vehicle was a larger pickup truck.

Her heart pounded and her palms grew slick against the wheel. She was driving fifteen miles over the speed limit and approaching another curve.

She tapped her brakes and the gap closed. A second later, a bump from behind thrust her vehicle forward. Her tires squealed and she struggled to keep the SUV on the road.

Coming out of the curve, she straightened the wheel

but didn't loosen her grip. If she could hang on until after the last curve, she could pull out her phone and call 911.

She floored the pedal, but the distance she gained quickly evaporated. The vehicle behind her slammed into her, snapping her head backward against the seat. She pressed the brake, but the truck pushed her into the next curve. After a prolonged squeal, her tires gave up their traction and the Escalade slid sideways. She bounced several times, her head snapping side to side.

Then the world started a slow spin. Her seat belt tightened against her legs and the airbag slammed into her. Pain shot through her face and one arm. A high-pitched scream filled the car. A terrifying moment passed before she realized it was hers.

The SUV came to rest at a sharp sideways angle. She pushed the airbag out of the way, her seat belt the only thing keeping her from tumbling to the passenger side of the vehicle.

She looked around in the darkness. Had her attacker fled, or was he making his way down the slope to finish what he'd started?

She wasn't going to wait to find out. After a quick check for broken bones, she pulled the handle and gave the door a hard shove. Small bits of window glass tumbled downward, but the door didn't budge. Using her shoulder didn't work, either.

After killing the headlights, she stared into the night. No one was approaching. The darkness wasn't complete, but it was close. She needed to get out of the vehicle. And she needed to call for help.

With her feet pressed into the floorboard and one hand gripping the wheel, she released the belt and eased into the passenger seat. She wasn't getting out that way, either. Her SUV rested against a large tree. It was what had kept her from continuing her tumble all the way to the bottom of the slope.

Where was her purse? She turned on the map lights, then crawled between the bucket seats. Both her purse and laptop were lying on the rear floorboard.

Her hands shook as she fished out her phone. After punching in the numbers, she pressed the phone to her ear.

As she relayed what had happened, she reached over the console to turn off the lights. She'd be safer sitting in the dark. With mobile locate, emergency personnel would find her. To make their job a little easier, she'd click on the headlights once she heard sirens.

When the dispatcher asked, she passed on the ambulance. She'd be sore tomorrow. But nothing was broken or dislocated. The airbag had even protected her from the shattered glass. She'd be free to leave after the police report. She'd take a cab to Murphy, and tomorrow morning, a wrecker would retrieve her car and tow it to a shop.

Meanwhile, she had time to think.

Why had someone gone after her? Was it a case of road rage? Maybe she'd cut someone off without realizing it, and they'd followed her from the interstate, irrational anger building with every passing mile.

If she had, she hadn't noticed. And who would wait more than an hour to react to someone cutting them off in traffic?

Another scenario was more likely. But it was one she didn't want to consider—that the attack might be personal.

A little more than a week ago, her parents had tumbled down a mountain to their deaths.

Tonight, she'd missed a curve, too, with a little help. Had her parents' brakes failed? Or had they gotten the same kind of nudge?

As much as she didn't want to think about it, the question wouldn't leave her alone.

THREE

Cooper darted to the next tree, while Bryce stood on his porch, flashlight beam pointed into the front yard. The dog wasn't in any hurry to take care of business.

A shiver shook Bryce's shoulders. He should have donned a jacket instead of stepping outside in the light sweater he wore. Friday's storm hadn't just brought hours of rain. It had also left some colder temperatures. And a tree down in Andi's front yard. During the next day or two, he'd get it cut up and hauled away.

"Hurry up, Cooper. I'm not standing here all night."

Cooper didn't acknowledge the command. Whatever smells he'd discovered were much too intriguing.

Bryce clapped his hands, and the dog's head swiveled toward him. A half second later, he was back to sniffing a browning clump of day lilies at the base of the tree.

With a sigh, Bryce stepped off the porch. "Come on, Cooper. Do your business."

The dog was much better behaved now than he'd been six months ago. Bryce had adopted him through Logan's Run, one of the rescue organizations in Murphy.

After spending the first two years of his life chained in someone's backyard, he'd needed a lot of love and care. Bryce had given it, and Cooper was now a different dog. He no longer moped around, head lowered. Instead of listlessness and disinterest, his eyes held enthusiasm.

Bryce glanced around the yard. Early that morning, a fat crescent had sat low on the eastern horizon. Now at 10:00 p.m., stars were scattered across a moonless night sky. Beyond the beam of his flashlight, everything was black. Except…

He drew his brows together as he stared into the woods that separated his property from Andi's. Light was coming from somewhere on the other side of the trees.

Was Matt snooping around again? Or had someone come back into her house?

Bryce stalked toward the dog. Cooper was finished, whether he thought he was or not. Apparently sensing his time to dally was over, the dog lifted a leg.

After leading him into the house, Bryce put on a jacket, then retrieved his weapon and phone. Moments later, he was on the trail connecting the two properties. It had gotten a lot of use when he and Andi were teenagers— summers and weekends, anyway. Since then, he'd maintained it so he could check on the property and visit with Dennis Wheaton.

Before he reached the end of the trail, he had no doubt. Someone was inside the house. Or *had* been. Last night, everything had been dark. Now the porch light was on, and light came from both the living room and her bedroom.

People up to no good usually didn't turn on lights. But whoever was there, it wasn't Andi. Her car wasn't in the driveway. Besides, he'd seen her a few hours ago. He hadn't made it to the graveside service, but he'd attended the funeral. It had been as packed as he'd expected. He'd sought her out afterward, weaving his way through the crowd. The conversation was like all her interactions with him—brief and polite, but lacking warmth.

He'd learned she was returning to work on Monday and had no idea when she'd make it back to Murphy. Her plans wouldn't have changed that fast. Andi wasn't the impulsive type. And knowing he was watching the place, if she was allowing someone to stay there, she would have mentioned it.

He jogged past the downed poplar, then slipped behind a hemlock. Drapes hung at the windows, a minuscule gap around their edges releasing slivers of light. A shadow moved past, and he pulled his phone from his pocket.

The intruder was still there, and Bryce wasn't reckless enough to confront him alone.

He called 911 and waited, keeping watch from behind the hemlock. Ten minutes later, the living room light went off. Maybe the intruder was preparing to leave.

His hand shifted to his weapon. He hadn't planned to confront anyone alone. But if someone emerged before backup arrived, he wouldn't hesitate.

The bedroom light was still on when sirens sounded a short distance away. He drew his weapon, covering the front door. As soon as the intruder realized police were coming, he'd probably take off. Out the back.

Bryce cast a glance over his shoulder, where a unit moved up the drive toward him, red and blue lights reflecting against the trees.

He stepped into the headlight beams and motioned his intentions. The bedroom curtains shifted to the side, then dropped back into place. The intruder was likely preparing to make a run for it. If he ran out the back,

Bryce would be ready. If he chose the front, the others would nab him.

Bryce had just settled into position when a loud knock reverberated through the night. He tightened his grip on the pistol. With the others in front, the intruder would surely use the back.

A deep male voice boomed. "Police. Open the door."

Bryce smiled. Sounded like Gary, one of his fellow deputies. Besides being armed, the man was two hundred and eighty pounds of solid muscle.

For the next minute, Bryce kept his ears peeled and his weapon trained on the back door. Finally, a soft female voice reached him from somewhere in front.

Wait, he recognized that voice. What was Andi doing there?

He lowered his weapon and jogged around the house. Gary was at the bottom of the porch steps, his partner Jason at his side. Andi stood above them, light from the outdoor fixture spilling over her. She'd already gotten ready for bed and was wearing flannel pajamas in a multicolored pattern.

He drew closer. Acrobatic cats? Yes, she was wearing images of cats doing cartwheels and back bends. He stifled a smile. The design was relaxed and playful. And surprisingly attractive on her. Andi was probably the only woman alive who could rock a pair of flannel pj's.

Her eyes shifted to him, then back to Gary. "What's going on?"

Bryce stopped next to his colleagues. "What are you doing here?"

Her brows rose. "This is my house."

"When I talked to you after the funeral, you hadn't planned to come back anytime soon."

"I changed my mind. And I didn't think about the fact you're watching the place. I should have called."

Gary cut in. "If everything's all right, we'll leave you two to your business."

Bryce nodded. "Sorry about the false alarm. She's already had one break-in."

"Not a problem."

He watched the men walk to the cruiser, then turned back to Andi. "How long are you staying?"

"A week or two, maybe longer. I don't know yet."

A week or two. Still too short of a time to restore any kind of friendship. But maybe it would be a start.

"If you need anything, let me know." Not that she would. He'd probably be the last one she'd ask for help.

She gave him a stiff nod. The porch light was behind her, casting her face in shadow, but something didn't look right. A bruise seemed to be forming on one cheek, abrasions on the other.

He climbed the two steps and turned her to face him. Yeah, something definitely wasn't right.

"What happened to your face?"

"I got slapped by the airbag."

His chest clenched. "You were in an accident?" That explained her car not being in the driveway. "What happened?"

She turned and walked inside. Since she didn't shut the door in his face, he assumed it was all right to follow. By the time he closed and locked the door, she was sitting on the couch, feet tucked under her.

He eased into the recliner adjacent to her. "I'm guessing your car's not drivable, since it's not here."

"I don't know yet. It's still sitting somewhat sideways, propped up by a tree. It rolled at least once. In the morning, some tow-truck driver is going to have to figure out how to get it back up onto the road."

His gut tightened. "You ran off the road?"

"With a little help. I was on the winding part of 60 before Mineral Bluff. Someone rammed me from behind and pushed me off the road at the next curve."

He clenched his fists. He didn't have to ask if she thought it was intentional. "Any idea who or why?"

"Not a clue. I'm director of marketing for a sporting goods manufacturer, hardly a position that makes lethal enemies. My ex doesn't even have it in for me." She fell silent, brows drawn together. Her mind was probably following the same track his was.

He pushed himself to his feet and began to pace. "There are too many similarities between your parents' accident and what happened to you tonight. I don't think it's a coincidence."

What if Dennis Wheaton had gotten involved in something he regretted and created enemies, ones who were prepared to come after his daughter now that he was out of reach?

He stopped pacing. "How about staying with me until we get this figured out?"

She looked up at him through her lashes.

"Come on, you'd have your own space. It's a three-bedroom house." Of course, she knew that. She'd been there enough times. Back then, it had been his grandparents' place. Now they were living in one of those over-fifty-five communities with daily activities, his mother had remarried and the house belonged to him. And his mortgage company.

"I'll be all right here." She pursed her lips. "If someone is after me, how did they know I was coming? Until a few hours ago, I didn't know myself."

"Maybe someone followed you from Atlanta." It wasn't a comforting thought. He'd feel a whole lot better if she'd agree to stay with him.

He crossed his arms and leaned against the bookcase. "How did you get here?"

"A cab."

"I told you to call me if you needed anything."

She shrugged. "Why bother you when I could just as easily call a cab?"

"Your dad would have called me."

"I'm not my dad."

No, she wasn't. Formerly a straight-A student and a member of several clubs, she'd always been driven to succeed. But now she had a hard edge, a steely strength that probably served her well in the business world but kept people at arm's length. He'd always thought she took after her dad rather than her mother. Now he wasn't so sure.

He picked up a piece of paper that had been lying on the coffee table. "Your dad's note."

"I've been carrying it around in my purse and pulled it back out tonight, hoping everything would somehow come together." She rose to stand next to him, looking down at what he held.

"And did it?"

"The words are just as cryptic as when I first read them." Frowning, she took the paper from him. "He had a secret, something he kept buried deep inside. But there's no hint of what that secret might have been."

She laid the paper back on the table. "Whatever it was, he didn't take his life over it."

Bryce lifted his brows. Had she learned something new?

"My dad wasn't driving. When they were ready to leave the lodge, he wasn't feeling well. So my mom agreed to drive."

"He didn't kill himself." A burden Bryce had carried for the past several days slowly lifted, and a smile climbed up his cheeks.

"He didn't." A matching smile tugged at her own lips.

Bryce took her hands and squeezed, and for several moments, the tension between them dissolved. Then she pulled away, turning her back to him.

He heaved a sigh. If he hoped to restore any kind of amicable friendship with Andi, he'd have to find a way to atone for his past mistakes. But where could he start?

"I'm sorry," he said. "For everything. I know I messed up. I knew it the moment you walked up and saw——"

She raised a hand, cutting him off. She hadn't given him an opportunity to explain then and wasn't going to now, either. "It's over. All of that was a lifetime ago."

She was right. Going back to what they had was impossible. It wasn't even what he wanted. If she knew that, would it make a difference? Maybe he needed to just lay out his expectations.

He took a seat on the couch. "I don't know the details, but I know you've recently been burned. I've been through the wringer myself, and frankly, I don't have the energy to put into a relationship. So you can rest assured that I won't be pushing you toward anything that would make you uncomfortable."

She sat on the love seat and he continued.

"If we're going to live next door to one another, even on a temporary basis, I hope you'll let me be your friend. At least a concerned neighbor."

Some of the tension fled her features, and she dipped her head. "Sounds fair."

Relief flooded him. "I've gotten so used to watching this place and doing odd jobs that it's going to be a hard habit to break. I hope you'll let me continue."

"That's not necessary. Anything I don't want to do myself, I can hire someone."

The stiffness that had characterized their interactions the past several days was gone. But she projected a self-sufficiency and determination he didn't remember being there twelve years earlier.

She crossed one leg over the other and began swinging it in circles. The movement drew his gaze downward.

Andi had cute feet, small enough to fit into the size shoe stores always displayed. When she was younger, her toenails were a work of art, sometimes with lines, curves and geometric shapes in varying colors, sometimes painted to resemble some kind of fruit or other object.

Tonight, they were a single shade of pink. That carefree fancy she'd displayed as a teenager seemed to be buried deep. If it was still there at all.

Andi had changed. It wasn't just that she'd grown up. Life had knocked her around. Whatever damage living with her mother had done, her ex-husband had added to it. Dennis had had nothing good to say about the man.

Knowing how badly he'd hurt Andi, Bryce didn't, either. In fact, he wouldn't mind throwing a few punches.

He inwardly flinched at the hypocritical thought.

Sure, the other man had added to the wall around Andi's heart.

But his own thoughtless actions had laid the foundation.

* * *

Andrea's eyes shot open. She lay stock-still, muscles drawn tight. Five seconds ago, she'd been dead to the world. Now she was wide-awake, every sense on alert. Had she heard something?

No, it was just stress, lingering effects from having been run off the road. She released a breath she hadn't realized she'd been holding and tried to slow her racing heart.

A crash came from somewhere inside the house and she stifled a gasp.

"Keep it down." The raspy whisper set her teeth on edge.

She threw back the covers and sprang from the bed. If she could close and lock the door, maybe she could escape through the window before they charged into the room.

The response came in the same hushed tone. "Why? Nobody's here."

Andrea stopped in her tracks. They didn't know she was there. If she didn't alert them to her presence, maybe she could hide till they left.

"We don't know that."

"You saw what happened. She's still back there on that slope. Or in a hospital bed."

"Just shut up and check the bedrooms."

Panic shot through her. She bounded back toward the bed, bare feet silent against the rugs covering the hardwood floor.

Heavy footsteps pounded closer, and she flipped the bedspread up over the pillow. It wasn't neat, but maybe the bed wouldn't look recently slept in.

As she snatched her purse from the nightstand, she

cast a glance over her shoulder. Light seeped in through the door opening, moving erratically. Someone was approaching with a flashlight.

She dropped to the floor and slid under the bed. Two seconds later, the door swung fully open.

"You check this room. I'll check the others. Then we'll start our search. Or pick up where we left off."

She held her breath while her pulse pounded in her ears. Had she left any hint that the house was occupied? Her purse and phone were under the bed with her. The two small suitcases were sitting in the corner.

But they were empty. As late as she'd gotten in, she hadn't planned to unpack until morning. But after Bryce's visit, trying to go immediately to sleep would have been pointless.

So she'd tucked her clothes away in the closet and dresser drawers and put her toiletries in the bathroom medicine cabinet. Nothing she'd brought with her was out.

Except her father's note. Where had she left it?

Before getting ready for bed, she'd picked it up from the coffee table and carried it into the bathroom. She'd never retrieved it after brushing her teeth. But that by itself wouldn't give away her presence.

Wood scraped against wood as a drawer slid open. A moment later, the clothes she'd put away tumbled to the floor. Contents of a second drawer followed, and then a third.

Andrea watched from her hiding place, pulling in silent breaths. The men in her house were the same ones who'd run her off the road. And the same ones she'd walked in on Wednesday night. This time, they'd tried to make sure she wouldn't be there to interfere with their search. What were they looking for? And why hadn't they come for it right after attacking her on 60?

Maybe they'd needed to swap vehicles. It would make sense. Driving around Murphy with a smashed front end would be risky, especially when the damage matched hers.

More clothing joined that already on the floor. Soon the entire contents of her dresser were strewn across her room. The closet door slid back on its track, and more items followed.

"Finding anything?" The question came from down the hall, no longer a whisper.

"Not a thing."

What were they looking for? Money? Jewelry? Were they simply opportunists, hitting vacant houses? Not likely, considering they'd run her off the road to keep her away. They were after something specific.

If only she could call for help. Her phone was inside her purse. But it wouldn't be safe to use it until the men left.

Her eyes widened. She couldn't make a call, but she could send a text. She could even receive one silently. She'd never turned the volume back up after the funeral.

Something crashed to the floor, and she flinched. That was her piggy bank.

"I said to keep it down. She's not here, but you don't want to alert that neighbor." The reprimand wasn't delivered in a whisper, but it was guaranteed to not carry outside the house. The man in the back seemed to be the one in charge.

She didn't recognize the voice. Not that she expected to. The words she'd heard so far seemed devoid of an accent. Definitely not Matt. Her antagonistic neighbor spoke in a lazy Southern drawl, infused with a hefty dose of arrogance.

"Whatevuh."

Definitely New England—Boston or maybe New York. Not much to go on, but every little bit helped.

A porcelain doll came down next. The intruder was clearing the top shelf of the closet, which meant he had his back to her.

She started to touch her phone, then hesitated. She couldn't risk it. With only the beam of his flashlight, he might notice the screen's glow.

More items hit the floor. Finally, he walked to the other side of the bed, and she turned her head. He'd stopped in front of the upholstered chair that sat in the corner. After tossing the seat cushion onto the floor, he flipped the chair onto its side. The nightstand followed.

He circled back around and kicked several items out of the way. Some of the tension seeped out of her. He was finally finished. As soon as he left the room, she'd text Bryce.

Instead, he approached where she lay. Her heart pounded harder with every step. *Please don't look under the bed.*

He stopped, his feet inches away. A glove-covered hand reached down. The flashlight shone in her face. Her heart stopped. She closed her eyes and waited. Was he going to call the other guy or kill her himself?

He didn't do either. Instead, he stepped backward with a grunt. There was a long *shhhh* and a thud as he dragged her mattress off the box spring and tossed it to the floor. The flashlight beam swung around, and she tried to blink away the blind spot in the middle of her field of vision.

For the next minute or so, the light swept back and

forth, illuminating the piles of stuff on the floor. Then he walked from the room.

Andrea emitted an almost audible sigh of relief. He hadn't looked under the bed. Now she could text Bryce. He probably wouldn't see it till morning, but it was worth a shot.

The screen lit up. She scrolled to their last call and pressed the text icon. Flat on her stomach, with her head turned at a sharp angle, she had only one hand available. But she'd make it work.

Her thumb slid over the digital keypad as she typed out a short message.

Someone's in my house.

The man retreated down the hall, toward the master bedroom, and she pressed the send icon.

The footsteps stopped. "Done in that room."

"You checked everything?"

"I did. The dresser drawers, the closet."

"The underside of the drawers? Inside the dresser itself, behind the drawers?"

"Yeah, the dresser and nightstand. Nothing taped there."

"What about under the bed?"

Sirens blared in her head, drowning out the man's response. He *didn't* look under the bed, or he would've found her.

And within moments, he'd do just that.

Her heart pounded, sending blood roaring through her ears. She belly-crawled toward the other side of the bed. Heavy footsteps moved closer. She scurried to the overturned chair and ducked behind it as the flashlight beam swept the room.

The man emitted a series of grunts. He'd apparently lowered himself to the floor. The beam of light illuminated the area to her right. She expelled the air in her lungs and hugged her legs more tightly.

Then the light shifted to her left. For several tense moments, it didn't move. Had he seen her? Was she not completely hidden by the chair?

He rose with another long grunt, leaving the flashlight on the floor. There were more sounds of exertion, some scrapes and clunks and groans. What was he doing?

The direct light disappeared, becoming a distant glow. Finally, he walked from the room, once again leaving her in total darkness.

"Under the bed is clear." He was moving away, his footsteps and voice growing softer. "I even checked the bottom of the box spring. Nothing."

The response was a soft murmur. If both men were occupied in the master bedroom, maybe she could make it to the front door without being seen.

No, it was too risky. The one man might still be in the hallway. He'd already thoroughly searched her room and had no reason to go back in. As badly as she wanted to call for help, she was safest staying right where she was.

She peeked around the chair and craned her neck to look at the clock on the nightstand. It was 2:34 a.m. If the men planned to search the entire house as thoroughly as the one had searched her room, it was going to be a long night. Her muscles were already protesting the cramped position. She arched her back, then twisted side to side. It didn't help. Neither did leaning against the wall.

Finally, they moved back down the hall and stopped outside her door.

"You do this bathroom. I'll work on the kitchen. He hid it here somewhere. We're not giving up till we find it."

Who hid something? And why hide it in the house?

Because it was essentially abandoned. The weekly visits she and her dad had made years ago had turned semimonthly and monthly after she'd stopped coming. In the past two years, her dad's visits were even less frequent than that. If not for Bryce's diligence, the place would probably have had the windows broken out and become a hangout for the Matts of the area to get high.

Whatever the men were looking for, it couldn't be related to her father. He'd always lived an uneventful, straightforward life. He was an accountant and financial planner. One couldn't get much more boring than that.

"Hey, check this out." The voice belonged to the New Englander. He'd probably found the paper. "He buried it."

The other man joined him. "'When a secret is too heavy to keep, it's always best to bury it deep.'" He paused. "Keep looking. The boss is going to expect us to eliminate every possibility that it's hidden inside first."

Andrea frowned. They had it all wrong. That was her dad's handwriting. Nothing was physically buried. The meaning was figurative. Surely they didn't plan to do to the yard what they were doing to the house.

One of the men tromped back toward the kitchen, while the other resumed his work in the bathroom. As bottles of makeup, cleansers and other items hit the Formica countertop, Andrea cringed. The glass door on the medicine cabinet banged shut, and the wooden one below the sink creaked open. Cleaners tumbled out while the clink and clatter of dishes came from the kitchen. At least the one out there wasn't throwing everything to the floor like this guy had.

A plastic bottle tumbled into the hall, likely kicked. "Nothing in here."

"Check the living room. We've got to find it before his kid gets her hands on it."

Andrea gasped. *His kid.* Were they talking about her father after all? That didn't make sense. There had to be another explanation.

The New Englander continued, "There's a shed out back. You want me to search that while you finish inside?"

"I wouldn't think he'd hide something this important outside, but Dennis Wheaton was a smart man. What better hiding place than where no one would think to look?"

Andrea's stomach clenched. Her dad had hidden something, and the men were determined to find it before she did. Had he taken something that belonged to someone else, something valuable? That didn't sound like him at all.

Maybe he found something incriminating during one of his audits. If that were the case, he'd call the authorities and turn over what he had. He'd never hold on to something for blackmail. And what other purpose could there be?

Soon thuds came from the living room. For what seemed like the twentieth time, Andrea looked at the clock. It was a little after three thirty. Time *was* moving. Just barely.

By the time she heard the back door open and close, it was almost four o'clock. Had the guy checking the shed come back in, or had the other one finished and joined him outside?

She crawled from her hiding place and tiptoed toward the hall. Everything was quiet. Now she could phone for help. She placed the call and returned to her room to wait.

Had the men found what they were looking for?

If not, did they think she had it? How desperate were they to get it? They'd sounded pretty determined. Based on what she'd heard, they weren't likely to give up their search. Which meant they'd probably be back.

Or maybe they *had* found it. Maybe her dad had hidden it in the shed, or the living room, and that was why they'd left when they had.

What could her father have hidden? Something had been weighing on him. She'd known that for a long time.

Then he'd contacted Bryce. How had Bryce put it? He'd sounded like a man ready to unload a heavy burden. That burden he'd carried, the object he'd hidden and the situation he'd wanted to talk to Bryce about, were they all related?

She'd probably never know. Her heart twisted at the thought of anything tarnishing the memory of her sweet, loving father. If she didn't learn the truth, the unanswered questions would forever torment her.

She'd always been inquisitive. Her dad had encouraged it. Her mother hadn't.

But maybe her mother had been right. In this case, knowing wouldn't change a thing. It certainly wouldn't bring them back. Sometimes it was better to leave well enough alone, no matter how badly she wanted to do otherwise.

One of her mother's favorite sayings rang in her ears—
Curiosity killed the cat.

FOUR

A shrill whining sounded in the distance, and Bryce pulled the spare pillow over his head. It didn't help. If anything, the annoying noise grew louder.

Tossing the pillow aside, he opened one eye. Darkness shrouded his room; the only thing visible was the glowing red numerals on his digital alarm clock. It was 4:23 a.m. What was going on?

He bolted upright in bed. That was a siren. And it wasn't out on the four-lane. It was right there on Ranger Road.

His pulse jumped to double time as he swiped his phone from the nightstand. He had one text message, from Andi, sent at 2:21 a.m. Someone was in her house.

He sprang from the bed. Sixty seconds later, he was running out the door, fully dressed and armed. The siren died mid-screech, leaving an oppressive silence blanketing the night.

The red-and-blue glow dancing through the trees dimly lit the trail, and he stumbled forward at a half jog. Andi had to be safe. She'd been able to call for help, so she wasn't incapacitated.

But first she'd tried to contact *him*. Just as he'd encouraged her to do. And he hadn't responded. If she was hurt, he'd never forgive himself. As soon as he got back home, he was going to assign a different alert for notifications, something much more obnoxious than the single short buzz he currently had.

He broke from the tree line in time to see Gary disappear around the side of Andi's house. His partner, Jason, stepped onto the porch and rang the bell. Bryce crossed the yard at a full run and greeted his fellow deputy as the door swung inward.

Andrea stood in the opening, still wearing the cat pajamas. But this time fuzzy slippers adorned her feet, and her hair had obviously not seen a brush since sometime yesterday. It was flat on one side and poufy on the other. Her usually feathery bangs jutted upward at all kinds of interesting angles.

And he wanted nothing more than to wrap her in his arms and kiss her.

Jason stepped toward her. "Deputy Vining. We met briefly last night. You had—" he paused as his gaze flicked past her "—a home invasion?"

Andi moved back, swinging the door wider. Bryce's jaw dropped along with his heart. Someone hadn't just come inside. He'd completely trashed the place.

Jason walked into the living room and looked around. "Tell me what happened."

"I woke up to two men inside the house, ransacking everything."

"Any idea who they were?"

She shook her head. "One had a New England accent. The other didn't have any accent at all. I didn't know either of them."

Bryce listened as Jason continued with his questions.

As before, Andi had no idea who had broken in or what they were after. But any hopes he'd had that the first break-in was random died a quick and sure death. Dennis had something someone wanted. He'd apparently hidden it, and the intruders were determined to get their hands on it before Andi did.

"Would you like us to dust for prints?" The question came from Gary.

"It's not necessary in the first bedroom or the bathroom. The man who searched those rooms was wearing gloves."

Jason lifted a brow. "You saw his hands?"

"I was hiding under the bed. He bent down and laid the flashlight on the floor, inches from my face. I thought for sure he was going to check under there and find me."

She looked past Jason and met Bryce's gaze, the terror of that moment still lingering in her eyes. His chest clenched.

But the hug he longed to give her would be pushing the boundaries of the tentative friendship she'd agreed to. She'd likely stiffen and turn away. Not a scene he wanted to play out in front of Gary and Jason. He considered both men his friends. Having lived in Murphy all his life, he had dozens.

But there were friends, and there were *friends*, that small handful of people one connected with on a deeper level. For him that was Colton and Tanner. He hadn't shared all the details, but his friends knew there'd once been someone special and that he still kicked himself for having been young and stupid. Almost a decade of bonding during wilderness hikes, white-water rafting trips and rock climbing expeditions had a way of peeling away the barriers guys usually held on to.

By the time Jason and Gary left, they had a pad full of notes and a whole slew of prints that Bryce hoped belonged to someone other than Andi and Dennis. He wasn't counting on it, though. If the New Englander was wearing gloves, the other man probably was, too.

Bryce closed the front door and stood the bookcase back up, returning it to its place against the wall. Andi sank onto the couch. She didn't just look tired. She looked defeated.

He eased down next to her. "I'm sorry I didn't call someone for you. I didn't hear your text. I woke up to the sirens."

"Don't apologize. I couldn't risk the intruders hearing me call 911, so I tried shooting off a quick text. I knew it was a long shot." She released a slow breath, her body seeming to deflate with the action.

He lifted a hand to squeeze her shoulder. "I'll help you put all this back."

She didn't shrug off his touch. "I can handle it. I need to do some sorting anyway. If I decide to sell the place, I'll need to figure out what to do with everything."

If I decide to sell the place. Those words bothered him more now than the first time he'd heard them. A few hours ago, he'd assured her he wanted nothing more than friendship. Maybe *he* was the one who needed convincing. Through one casual relationship after another, he'd never been able to forget her. Even throughout his time with Pam, Andi had still held a piece of his heart.

Now she'd unexpectedly come back into his life. He'd treat it as the gift that it was and simply enjoy her friendship. He'd be insane to consider anything more. If her ex came to his senses and decided he wanted her back, he hoped Andi would tell him to take a hike. But he couldn't count on it. After all, the last thing he'd expected was for Pam to return to her abusive ex-boyfriend. People did foolish things in the name of love.

Andi released a sigh. "The men who broke in are the same ones who ran me off the road. They think my dad physically buried something."

"Is that what you think?"

"I don't know. Something was bothering him. That note he left confirms it. Between that and his conversation with you right before he died, I can't help thinking he was in some kind of trouble."

"I'm thinking the same thing." Whatever the trouble, the man had tried to enlist his help. Unfortunately, the accident had happened before he'd had a chance to tell anyone what was going on.

"What if he was involved in something illegal?"

"That doesn't sound like the Dennis Wheaton I know." When Bryce had been headed toward a life of crime alongside Matt, Dennis was the one who'd guided him onto the right path. "As well as I knew your dad, thinking he'd done something illegal is too much of a stretch."

She wanted to believe him. It was there in her eyes. "If anyone had suggested it two weeks ago, I'd have defended him with my dying breath. Now I have too many unanswered questions."

Her gaze dropped to the mound of stuff covering the floor. "My dad has always been successful, by most people's standards. But it was never good enough for my mother. Most of the money that supported our high standard of living came from her family. And she never let my dad forget it. I'm sure she loved him at one point, maybe still did at the end of her life. But it always seemed like he was a disappointment to her."

She rested her head against the back of the couch and closed her eyes. "When I was young, she was always pushing him to run for public office. Her grandfather and both brothers were politicians, and she had high aspirations for my dad. But he didn't want any part of it. Maybe if he'd agreed to be a public figure, the rest wouldn't have been so important."

She continued, fatigue creeping into her voice. "A year ago, things started to change. My dad seemed to have a lot more money. He and two partners started a financial planning business a few years ago. He attributed his success to the fact that the business was finally taking off, that they'd gained some high-profile clients."

She lifted her head and turned pain-filled eyes on him. "I never questioned it. I was just glad that my mother had finally stopped berating him. But what if the allure of making the kind of money she demanded finally overpowered his own honesty and integrity?"

Bryce tightened his fingers into a fist, his heart breaking for the man who'd had such an impact on his life. Continually criticized and made to feel like a failure. If he'd gotten involved in something shady, Bryce could almost understand. But not Dennis Wheaton. There had to be another explanation.

"We'll get to the bottom of this. When we do, we'll find out that your father died the same honorable man we've always loved and respected." He'd cling to that conviction with everything he had, unless they uncovered irrefutable evidence to the contrary. Even then, he'd be searching for an alternative explanation.

"I hope you're right." She pursed her lips. "I need to get into my dad's office. His partners have probably divvied up his clients, but no one will have a problem with me gathering up his personal items."

His chest tightened. "How about if I go with you?"

"That's not necessary."

"How well do you know his partners?"

"Somewhat. I've met them. Talked to them several times. Why?"

"Your dad had something. You don't know what or where he got it. So you don't know who you can trust. At this point, it would be safest to trust no one."

Worry wove through her features, leaving fine creases between her eyebrows. "That's going to make it hard to find out what my dad might have been involved in."

"Just be careful who you talk to and what you say. You're not supposed to know that your dad hid something. You certainly don't want anyone to know you were there when the two men broke in and could possibly identify them by their voices. All you know is that someone ransacked the house."

She nodded. "I'll be careful. I won't say anything, and if anyone asks, I'll play dumb. I need to go through my dad's office at home, too. Maybe I'll box everything up and bring it here."

"Which leads us to something else." He geared himself for a fight. She wasn't going to like what he had to say. "You shouldn't stay here alone."

She cast him the same doubt-filled glance she'd given him when he first suggested she stay at his place. "You're not moving in here. Those guys already overturned every square inch of this house. Why would they come back? I seriously doubt they'll be digging up my yard, even if they think something's buried here. Besides, they may have already found what they were looking for."

"You can't count on that. Let me sleep on your couch. I won't bother you. If these guys come back, hiding under the bed hoping they don't find you isn't a good plan."

"I'll get an alarm and have it monitored."

That was better. But it would still take the police fifteen or twenty minutes to get there. "If you won't let me stay, then at least let me loan you Cooper."

"Who's Cooper?"

"My dog."

"Oh, no. I'm not a dog person. I wasn't raised with them. You know what my mom always said? 'A dog is a man's best friend. A fur-free house is a woman's best friend.'"

Yeah, from his brief introduction to Mrs. Wheaton, that sounded like something she'd say. Her "fur-free house" principle probably extended to cats, too. As far as he knew, Andi had never had a pet, even a goldfish.

"Cooper's short-haired. He doesn't shed much, and certainly not this time of year. I'll get him in the morning and bring him back in the evening. You won't even have to feed him. He'd at least alert you if someone was prowling around outside."

She pursed her lips. Maybe she was considering the proposal. "He's not one of those yippy ankle biters, is he?"

"No, he's a black Lab. And he's got a pretty deep bark. He'd make a good guard dog." At least Bryce hoped he would.

"And he sleeps the night through? Doesn't ask to go out at 3:00 a.m.?"

"He never bothers me."

"He's not going to expect to sleep with me, right?"

"He has his own bed. I have it in my room, but I'm sure he'll be fine wherever you put him."

"All right. I'll give it a shot. You can bring him over tonight." She rose from the couch. "This afternoon, I'll see about getting a rental car, then pick up some groceries. But right now, I need more sleep than the little I've had so far."

"Not here. You can't even secure the place." The intruders had gained entry through the back door. According to Gary and Jason, screwdriver gouges marred the jamb, and the knob looked like it had tangled with the business end of a pipe wrench. "You can finish the night in my spare bedroom. I've even got clean sheets on the bed."

"Sounds good."

He lifted a brow. That was easier than expected. But Andi seemed to no longer have the energy to fight him. Now that the immediate crisis was over, fatigue was setting in fast. Her shoulders drooped and her eyelids grew heavier with every passing moment.

At least for the next few hours, she'd be safe. He'd make sure that her house was secure before nightfall. And he'd contact Tri-State Life Safety about the security system. Or see that Andi did.

Cooper would be standing guard at night. And within an hour, his cell phone was going to be programmed with the most obnoxious text alert he could find. By the end of today, he would've done everything he could.

As Andi said, maybe the intruders found what they wanted and wouldn't be back. But she wouldn't be willing to leave it at that.

As long as he'd known her, she'd been inquisitive. It

was one of the things that had made her such a good student and fueled her love of astronomy.

What she was after now wasn't some interesting piece
of knowledge. It was personal. Her father's memory was
at stake.

If he knew Andi, she wasn't going to give up until
she'd overturned every stone. She'd learn what had
weighed so heavily on her father.

Regardless of who tried to sway her otherwise.

Andrea pushed the cart through the produce section
at Ingles. Lettuce, tomatoes and cucumbers were stacked
in one end. Since she was going to be staying in Murphy
for some time, she needed to stock the fridge and pan-
try with more than milk, a box of cereal and some soup.

After adding carrots, apples and avocados, she wheeled
her cart away from produce. In another twenty minutes,
she'd be through her shopping. She glanced at a woman
moving toward her, then turned to head down a canned
goods aisle.

"Andi, is that you?"

Her cart screeched to a halt. She didn't get a good
enough look at the woman to recognize her, but she'd
know that sweet Southern drawl anywhere.

"Angie." They'd been casual friends but lost touch
once Andrea stopped coming to Murphy.

Angie parked her cart against the end cap and stepped
around it to give Andrea a hug, both of them bending to
accommodate a large baby bump.

Angie stepped back, holding her at arm's length. "You
look great. I haven't seen you guys in forever. Is your
dad with you?"

Andrea winced. If she was going to go through this

with every person she ran into, she might just lock herself inside the house and never come out.

"My parents were killed in a car accident. I'm here figuring out what to do with the house."

Angie's eyes widened. "I'm so sorry. I really liked your dad. He was always so nice."

Yeah, that seemed to be everyone's sentiment. Was there a side of him no one saw, including herself?

She redirected her thoughts. "You look like you're doing well." Angie had always been cute, but six or seven months pregnant, she radiated joy. Life had apparently turned out well for her.

"I'm married, expecting our second child." She rested a hand on her stomach. "I've got a party supply store and do special-events decorating. But I'm trying to sell my business so I can be a full-time mom."

"I hope it works out."

After chatting for a few more minutes, Angie returned to her cart. "I'll let you get back to your shopping. If you were planning to stay, I'd try to talk you into taking over my business. With your artistic ability, you'd be really good at it." She laughed. "You'd hardly even have to change the name. It could be Designs by Andi instead of Designs by Angie."

Andrea waved away the compliment. Whatever artistic ability she'd once had had lain dormant for so many years it was well past the point of resurrection. Her mom had never encouraged anything that didn't further Andrea's climb up the social or corporate ladder.

Phil hadn't expressed an opinion one way or the other. But most of their married life, she'd been too busy putting him through medical school to pursue anything more frivolous than sleep. Once he finished his residency, she'd kept up the pace. Giving 140 percent was a hard habit to break.

Andrea finished her shopping and headed out the automatic doors. Her rental car waited in the parking lot, a dark blue Honda Accord. She'd agreed to let Bryce take her to pick it up. Her own vehicle was at a body shop, where the wrecker had towed it. Her insurance adjuster would look at it sometime this week.

Though she'd let Bryce give her a ride to town, she'd turned him down when he'd insisted on helping put the house back in order. He didn't need to spend his day off working at her place. She'd rather be alone for the task, anyway. Sorting through her dad's possessions wasn't going to be easy. Too many things in that house had memories attached.

After leaving her empty cart in one of the corrals, she climbed into the Accord. A stack of mail sat in the seat next to her, the first of many thank-you notes she'd be writing for flowers and donations made to her parents' favorite charities. They wouldn't leave the post office till tomorrow, but she may as well deposit them while she was out.

Then she could head for home. She'd managed to tackle the kitchen and part of the living room before picking up the rental car. This afternoon and evening, she'd see how far she could get on the rest of it. She also needed to call a tree company tomorrow to take care of the downed poplar. She was surprised Bryce hadn't insisted on doing it.

Finding out he had no interest in renewing a romantic relationship had been a relief. She couldn't deny that the spark was still there. But it didn't matter. Anything deeper than friendship was out of the question.

It wasn't because he'd broken up with her years ago, saying he thought they should date other people. It was because she'd found him less than two hours later making out with a friend of theirs. Based on what she'd seen, it hadn't been the first time. So much for *always and forever*.

She drove from the parking lot and stopped at the traffic light, waiting to cross the four-lane. Next to her, an array of Christmas trees occupied the field at the corner, for sale by the Rotary Club.

The light changed, and she stepped on the gas, her chest tightening. Christmas was three and a half weeks away. She'd been dreading this one, her first holiday season as a divorcée. It was also going to be her first holiday season without her parents. A double whammy. If she could figure out a way to go to sleep on December 23 and not wake up until December 26, she'd do it.

But that wasn't an option. She'd face the upcoming holiday the same way she'd faced everything else life had thrown at her the past several months. She squared her shoulders and then let them fall. All the determination in the world wasn't going to fill the emptiness that had taken up residence inside.

She crossed a bridge and pressed the brake. On the left stood a small church with white stucco walls and a steeple topped by a cross. The post office was just past it. She dropped her mail into the box, then pulled back onto Andrews.

As she passed the church again, she looked at it more closely. A small sign on the side said Free Methodist Church. At twelve thirty, the service was probably over, but several cars still occupied the parking lot. Small and simple, it looked like just the kind of place her mother had warned her about.

And exactly where she needed to be.

Something tugged at her, a longing she couldn't identify. Maybe she could find it inside. Maybe her church back home had had it, too, and she'd just been too preoccupied to see it.

She glanced in her right-side mirror, which framed the image of the little white church. Next week she'd go. She'd even see if Bryce wanted to attend, if not this one, the one they'd gone to years ago. That church had been small, too, filled with people who were warm and friendly, without pretense.

She traveled back to the four-lane and headed for home. As she snaked her way up Ranger Road some time later, she glanced left, then wished she hadn't. Matt was out front, blowing leaves from the Langman drive. He stopped to stare at her as she passed, eyes narrowed.

She'd gotten the same glare from him when she'd ridden by a couple of hours earlier in the front passenger seat of Bryce's Sorento. Matt's dad had apparently put him to work doing chores and he wasn't happy about it.

Or maybe he just wasn't happy to see that she'd come back.

Ignoring her neighbor, she rounded the next curve and turned onto her own property, stopping at the mailbox. After arriving so late last night, she hadn't thought to check it.

She shifted her gaze toward the house and heaved a frustrated sigh. If there *was* any mail, it would wait.

Bryce stood in profile, gripping a chain saw, safety glasses shielding his eyes. As she made her way up the gravel drive, a high-pitched whine seeped through the car's closed windows, growing louder as she approached.

When she stepped from the car, he killed the saw's motor and pulled a foam plug from one ear, letting it dangle from a plastic string.

She planted one hand on her hip. "What do you think you're doing?"

"Cutting up your tree."

"My trees are my responsibility."

He shrugged. "I have a chain saw. I figured I'd skip the objections and get started while you were gone."

"I was going to call someone first thing in the morning. Anything I can't do myself, I can afford to pay for."

"There's nothing wrong with being a good neighbor." He cranked the saw again and made another cut.

She shut the door and stalked toward him, waving both arms. He made it through two more cuts before looking up at her.

He killed the saw and lowered it to his side. "If it'll make you feel any better, I'll take some of the pieces for firewood."

"And you'll let me pay you." Bryce wouldn't demand anything in return, but she hated being obligated to anyone. And that was how she'd feel if he kept doing things for her.

A muscle worked in his jaw. "I don't need your money, Andi."

She winced at the coldness in his tone. The differences in their families' income and social status had never mattered to her. It had to him. Maybe he still hadn't gotten over it.

"I know you don't. But I was planning to pay someone." She gave him a weak smile. "I'm trying to not take advantage of your generosity."

"It's not taking advantage when I insist."

"Then let me at least help. I'll haul and stack logs. We'll split the firewood."

As she moved to retrieve her groceries, a white Lexus turned into the drive.

Bryce stepped closer, the action protective. "Are you expecting someone?"

"No."

The car came to a stop behind the Accord. The driver's door swung open and a businessman climbed out. At least, that was what she assumed he was. He looked to be in his midfifties, dressed in typical business attire: dark suit, pale blue shirt and a striped tie. With a receding hairline and a paunch that spoke of too many hours behind a desk, the guy looked harmless enough. But she was glad to have Bryce next to her.

The visitor stopped a few feet from where she stood and removed a business card from a metal holder. "I'm Melvin Drysdale with Choice Property Development." He cast a sideways glance at Bryce. "If this isn't a good time, I can come back."

Andrea took the card. "You can talk freely in front of Bryce. He's my neighbor and keeps an eye on the place."

"Pleased to meet you, Bryce. I'm here to hopefully relieve you of your responsibilities." He turned his attention back to Andrea. "My group would like to buy your property. I'm sure we can arrive at a price you'll be more than happy with."

She drew her brows together. "It's not even on the market. How did you know—"

"The obituary was in the paper. I'm sorry for your loss."

"Thank you. I haven't made a decision yet." She pocketed his card. "I'll get in touch with you if I decide to sell."

He looked around. "This is a lot of land to keep up, and the house is pretty run-down. Your life is in Atlanta. Do you really want to deal with all this?"

Uneasiness sifted through her. "How do you know where I live?"

"You're listed on the property appraiser's website as half owner."

"With my address?" Since the tax bills went to her father, probably not.

Drysdale shrugged. "I did my homework."

She crossed her arms. "This place has been in my family for generations." And no one was going to push her into making a decision before she was ready. "If I decide to sell, I'll contact you. Right now, it's too soon. I just buried my parents yesterday."

"I know it's difficult." He walked to his car and opened the door. Instead of getting in, he looked at her over the Lexus's roof. "Keep in mind, it's often easier to pick up the pieces and move on if we don't have unfinished business hanging over us."

She clenched her fists, struggling to hold on to her cool professionalism. "Tell me, Mr. Drysdale, have you ever had to pick up the pieces and move on?" She didn't give him a chance to respond. "I'm guessing not. If and when I decide to sell, I'll let you know. And the timing will be my decision."

Drysdale bobbed his head. "Yes, of course. Again, I'm

sorry for your loss. Take some time to get your bearings, then give me a call."

He got into the car, turned around and sped down the drive.

Once he pulled onto Ranger, Andrea released a sigh. "Did you get the same kind of vibes from him that I did?"

"What, the stubborn, sleazy, condescending ones?"

"Yeah, those."

"Totally." He gave her an encouraging pat on the back. "Don't let him pressure you into a decision you might later regret."

"I won't. I don't let people push me around." She gave him a wry smile. "Except my mother. Not many people had what it took to go up against her, not even my dad."

After putting away the groceries and changing into a sweatshirt and an old pair of jeans, she returned to the front yard, where more cut limbs had joined the others. "Have you checked the mail lately?"

"Not since the day before you first arrived. The regular mail lady knows not to put anything in the box, but sometimes a substitute will deliver the flyers and coupon papers."

She shrugged. She may as well check. There'd been four mail-delivery days since Bryce had last looked. She made her way down the drive, dried leaves crunching beneath her feet. Behind her, the saw started up, the pitch rising as Bryce pressed whirring metal blades to wood. Maybe she'd check the shed for some earmuffs. A pair of leather gloves, too.

When she reached the street, she waited for a car to pass. The driver raised a hand in greeting. Probably someone who lived farther up Ranger. She didn't know him. After having been gone twelve years, there'd be a lot of people she didn't know.

She stepped in front of the box and swung the metal door downward. Lifeless eyes stared back at her. Dried blood was caked around one side of the mouth. The rest of the furry body disappeared into the shadow of the box.

A scream shot up her throat, and she stumbled backward, hand over her mouth. Bryce continued working, his back to her. Leaving the box open, she stalked up the driveway, her initial shock pushed aside by anger. What she saw had Matt written all over it.

She circled Bryce and held up a hand. As soon as his eyes met hers, he killed the saw.

"What's wrong?"

"You need to look in the mailbox."

He laid the saw on the ground, then covered the distance at a jog. When he reached the box, his jaw clenched. "A dead squirrel in your mailbox. I would take this as a threat."

"Or someone trying to really annoy me. And I'm pretty sure I know who."

Bryce reached in to remove the dead animal, and she cringed. He was wearing gloves, but still. She watched him turn the body over and inspect it.

"I'm guessing it was hit by a car, then put in the box. It also happened recently enough that it hasn't started to decay. I'll toss it into the woods."

"Or bury it."

Vultures usually disposed of wildlife struck by cars, and that was okay. They were nature's cleanup crew. Death was part of life.

But this one bothered her—the thought that it might

have been killed intentionally, just to take vengeance on her.

She pressed a hand to the metal door to close it, then leaned down to look inside. She had mail after all, pushed toward the back. She reached inside the box and pulled it out.

It wasn't mail. At least it hadn't gone through the post office. There was no envelope, no address or stamp. Just a piece of notebook paper folded in thirds, "Andrea" printed across the outside.

Bryce's eyes widened. "Don't handle it."

She dropped it back into the box. After placing the squirrel on the ground, he retrieved and unfolded the sheet.

Andrea moved to stand beside him, her gaze sliding over the words. A block of ice settled in her stomach, chilling her all the way to her core.

This was no simple prank. It was a threat, no matter how much she wanted to believe otherwise.

She scanned the words again, darkness pressing down on her with each one—

"Being where you don't belong can be deadly."

FIVE

Fire shot through Bryce's veins. This time Matt had crossed a line. "Come on."

Leaving the squirrel lying where he'd put it, he charged down the street with Andi right behind him. At the end of the Langman drive, Matt's old Charger sat near the house, front end jacked up, tools scattered around it. Matt was always tinkering. Everything he knew about mechanics he'd learned from his dad. But there was one big difference. Jimmy Langman had held a job at a garage in town for the past twenty years. Matt had never kept one more than two months.

Bryce climbed the porch steps and knocked loudly enough to be heard at the four-lane. While he waited, he looked around. Matt was nowhere to be seen, but several items belonging to either him or his dad littered the porch. A tattered jacket hung from the railing, and a pair of tennis shoes sat near the door. Gray with a neon green swish, they'd been classy at one point. Now they were worn and stained with grease.

When the door finally opened, Mr. Langman stood there scowling. "Stop all the racket already. What's the cotton-picking emergency?"

"Your son's been harassing Andi since she arrived, and it's going to stop now."

The old man's eyes shifted her direction and narrowed. "If she's going to threaten my boy for being on her property, she'd better stay off mine, or I'll trespass her."

"If that boy of yours keeps up the threats, he's going to jail. Andrea has inherited the property and has every right to enjoy it in peace."

Langman's bushy eyebrows lifted. "Inherited? Her old man's gone?" His nostrils flared. "Good riddance."

The final words were barely audible. But Andi's sharp intake of air said she'd heard them, too. No wonder Matt had such hatred for the Wheatons. He'd learned it from his father.

Matt stepped into the room and shuffled to the door. "What's wrong?"

Bryce locked gazes with his former friend. Matt knew exactly why they were there. The self-confident grin proved it. Bryce held up the paper and shook it. "The dead squirrel is pretty serious. But threats like this can land you in jail."

Matt shrugged, not even trying to read what was there. He didn't need to. He'd written it.

"I'm warning you. Stay away from her. And stay away from the Wheaton property."

"If you think it was me, prove it."

"I intend to."

He spun and stalked to where Andi waited at the bottom of the steps. He'd have taken her hand if he weren't still wearing the contaminated gloves. But he wasn't removing them until he had the note tucked into a plastic bag. Matt had probably worn gloves. But Bryce wasn't going to rule out the possibility of prints being left until the department did.

Andi headed down the drive next to him, fists clenched and eyes filled with determination. "This property has been in my family for four generations. If I decide to sell it, it'll be because I want to, not because some greedy property developer wants to get his hands on it or a nasty neighbor is trying to scare me away."

"Good for you."

He admired her spunk. And though he hoped she'd keep the property, he'd support her in whatever decision she made.

When she reached her driveway, she cast a glance at the squirrel lying at the base of the mailbox. Bryce bent to pick it up. If Andi wanted it buried, he'd get out the shovel and start digging.

As they walked toward the old house, Andi drew in a deep breath and released it in a sigh. "I'm usually a decisive person. I knew right away I was going to get rid of the place in Atlanta. My two-bedroom condo is plenty for me. Selling my parents' seven-thousand-square-foot house made total sense."

She continued around the side of the house. "The decision about this place is harder. Keeping it doesn't make much sense. I don't know that I'll even make it up here. But every time I think about letting it go, I feel sick."

"Why wouldn't you make it up here? You're only two hours away."

"My work schedule doesn't leave time for much else. Corporate America." She gave him a rueful smile. "But I enjoy what I do."

He frowned. "How many days a week do you work?"

"Usually six." She opened the door to the shed. "My

team works Monday through Friday. Saturday is my time to catch up on whatever I didn't get done that week and organize things for the next. Sunday, I do chores at home."

He watched as she fished through the lawn tools for a shovel. She'd always had enough ambition for five people. She'd graduated high school at the top of her class, with the goal of obtaining a graduate degree from one of the Ivy League schools. According to Dennis, she'd succeeded.

But the Andi of twelve years ago knew how to have fun and didn't mind taking time out for drawing, stargazing and hanging with friends.

Did she really love working that much? Or was there something else behind her desire to keep such an insane schedule?

He took the shovel she handed him and moved toward the edge of the woods. "Sometimes it's good to slow down, take time out for things you enjoy."

"I do. I mean, I don't work *all* the time."

"When's the last time you did something just for fun?"

"Thanksgiving."

"Holidays don't count. Before that."

"Six weeks ago."

He stopped just inside the tree line. After laying the squirrel on the decaying bed of leaves, he drove the shovel into the hard ground. "What did you do six weeks ago?"

"Took my team out for dinner."

"That's work."

"No, it's not."

"Okay. Tell me why you took them out. If I were to ask one of them that question, what would they say?"

"To reward them. We'd completed a big campaign."

"That's an employee incentive. Definitely falls into the category of work."

She crossed her arms and frowned up at him. "We were talking about my deciding whether or not to sell the property. How did we end up here?"

"You said you didn't know if you'd even have time to come up here and use this place, or something to that effect."

"Okay, so I did." She pursed her lips. "There's nothing wrong with being ambitious."

"No, there's not. But when people have too much ambition, they're workaholics." He slanted her a glance. "Anyone ever accuse you of that?"

"More than once. But in the corporate world, that's encouraged, even rewarded." She heaved a sigh. "Maybe I *do* need to keep this place. It'll force me to take time off and at least make occasional trips up. Otherwise, it wouldn't be practical to spend the money for upkeep. And I'm all about practicality." She paused. "So there's my decision."

He stopped his digging to look at her. "Just like that?"

"Just like that. I think I knew all along I wouldn't be able to bring myself to sell it. And I don't have to. I can keep up my condo in Atlanta and still afford the maintenance on this place." She leaned back against a tree, a relaxed smile touching her lips. "With that decision, I feel like a weight has been lifted off me."

Yeah, him, too. But it was more than that. Her decision had left him with a sense of elation that he had a hard time explaining, even to himself. Laughter bubbled just below the surface, clamoring to get out. If he let everything he was feeling flow, Andi would think he'd lost his mind.

But Andi was one of his oldest friends. Friends were important to him. Tanner was a mile away, over on 294, with his fiancée, Paige, in the cabin at the back of Tanner's property. Colton and Mandy lived a short distance the other direction, on Hilltop. And when Andi came up, she'd be right next door. All his closest friends within a one-mile radius.

That was the only reason for his giddiness.

He looked down at the shallow hole he'd dug. "If you want this any deeper, you'll have to get me a pickax."

"That's good. He's getting a better burial than he would've if he hadn't ended up in my mailbox."

Bryce laid the squirrel in the hole and scooped dirt over it. After packing it down, he spread dried leaves with the edge of one boot.

Andi lifted her shoulders and then let them fall. "Now that the decision's made, I guess I need to call Melvin Drysdale."

He walked to the shed and returned the shovel to its place against the side wall. "Want me to get rid of him for you?"

"I can handle him."

He had no doubt about that. She didn't get where she was without being able to handle people.

He followed her inside, where she retrieved the card Drysdale had given her and slid her phone from her back pocket. Ten or fifteen seconds after she punched in the number, a smile climbed up her cheeks. "Voice mail. I get to take the coward's way out."

Her message was short and sweet. She thanked him

for his interest but let him know she'd decided to keep the property.

"Another task knocked off my to-do list." She dropped the card in the trash. "In the last fifteen minutes, I've made the decision to keep the property and gotten rid of Drysdale. Now we're going to finish getting that tree out of my front yard. A productive afternoon, wouldn't you say?"

"Quite." He certainly had no complaints about how the day was shaping up. Any decisions that brought Andi back to Murphy on a semi-regular basis were good ones. And the longer she planned to stay on this trip, the better.

He also had her safety to think about. Even with a security system and Cooper standing guard, she wasn't totally safe at the old house. But better next door than two hours away.

Whatever trouble Dennis Wheaton had found, it probably didn't originate in Murphy. It likely followed him from Atlanta.

And if it followed Dennis from Atlanta, it could easily follow Andi back.

The tantalizing scent of chocolate chip cookies filled the kitchen. Andrea took the final tray from the oven and placed it on a rack to cool. One dozen was already sealed in a plastic container, with another dozen and a half on a plate covered with foil. She'd picked up ingredients when she'd been at Ingles, not intending to use them until she'd finished sorting through the house and putting everything away. But she'd accomplished enough in the yard this afternoon to justify goofing off.

Andrea returned the pot holders to the drawer and turned off the oven. She hadn't baked in years. She hadn't had the time. With a great bakery a few blocks from her condo, there'd been no need. But her purchases had never made her kitchen smell like this. If she was going to take up baking, she'd also have to get a gym membership. Her promise to indulge in only one cookie had fallen by the wayside. She'd polished off three before finally sealing up the container.

But she was giving away the rest. Now that she'd decided to keep the property, she'd be hiring a handyman to help with projects. The cookies would be a bonus.

She shrugged into her jacket, then picked up the foil-covered plate, which was still warm. That one was going to Bryce. He'd never let her dad pay him, and he wasn't letting her pay him, either. But no man turned down homemade chocolate chip cookies.

After taking a flashlight from the drawer, she opened the front door. The porch light spilled over the yard in a semicircular glow, holding back a wall of darkness. She locked the door behind her and pocketed the key. At seven in the evening, no one was likely to be prowling around, but it never hurt to be cautious.

After picking her way along the trail, she stepped into Bryce's yard and stopped, memories bombarding her. His porch light was on. A swing hung from the roof at one end. How many hours had they spent sitting there, talking and laughing, sharing kisses in the moonlight?

But those weren't the images that played through her mind. Only one was there, stuck on pause: Bryce with Carla sitting in his lap, arms entwined around one another—

She forged ahead, refusing to dwell on the past. It happened twelve years ago. They'd barely been adults. What she'd experienced six months ago had been so much worse. Bryce's betrayal shouldn't even still bother her.

But it did. Eighteen or thirty, age didn't matter. Betrayal stung regardless.

She shook off the thoughts and climbed his porch steps. Deep-throated barks answered her knock. Bryce was right. Cooper would be a good guard dog. She'd go ahead and bring him home when she left. She still wasn't thrilled with the arrangement. But it made Bryce feel better. And it was only temporary.

The door swung inward, and Bryce frowned down at her. "What are you doing here?"

"Uh, cookies?" She'd expected a little friendlier greeting.

"You shouldn't venture out alone after dark." The frown was still there. "If you do have to go outside for something, please call me."

"Okay, I will." He was overreacting. Someone was on a treasure hunt. No one had tried to hurt her. Well, they had, out on 60, but that was to keep her away from the house while they did their search. Now that was done.

His gaze dipped to what she held, and his expression softened. "Come in."

After taking the plate, he drew in a slow breath and peeked under the foil. "You made these?"

"Yep. Just now."

He picked up one and took a large bite. "Mmm, my favorite. You remembered." He closed the door behind her. "Thank you."

The smile he gave her did funny things to her insides. Yes, she remembered. Chocolate chip had always been his favorite. Not only had she made them for him on several occasions. They'd also made them together.

A sudden sense of nostalgia struck her, along with an awareness of something lost, precious moments that could never be regained.

She cleared her throat and looked down at the dog, who appeared to be having a hard time containing himself. He kept shifting his weight from one side to the other, his tail wagging at a furious pace.

Bryce grinned. "Andi, meet Cooper."

"Hello, Cooper." Andrea held out a hand.

Bryce patted the dog's back. "Shake."

Cooper lifted a paw toward his master.

"Not me, silly. Shake Andi's hand."

He continued to paw Bryce's jean-clad leg.

"We're still working on some of the commands. But he's doing great, considering where he was when I got him. Six months ago, you'd have rather taken your chances with an ax murderer than share a house with him. I ended up replacing a great pair of hiking boots, along with some belts and a uniform, after he reallocated them for chew toys." He ruffled the fur behind the dog's neck. "This guy did more for getting me to pick up after myself than eighteen years of my mom's nagging."

She laughed, bending to pet the dog. When she straightened, she glanced around the room. The furniture had been changed to something more modern than what his grandparents had had, and the walls were now a toned-down mustard color instead of antique white.

But that wasn't what had snagged her gaze and held it. It was the five framed sketches hanging over the living room couch—each drawn by her. Two were portraits, one of her dad and one of Bryce. The others were scenes of activities they'd shared together—a visit to Hiwassee Dam, stargazing on her own back deck, Bryce leaning against the old well. Her dad must have given him the sketches sometime after she'd left and Bryce had had them matted and framed.

And kept them displayed. Had he simply appreciated the artwork? Or had he felt something for the artist all these years?

He grinned down at her. "There probably aren't many people who own a collection of early Andrea Wheaton originals."

She returned his smile. "No, you're the only one."

"Have you continued with your artistic endeavors?"

"Not unless you count choosing the color scheme and furnishings for my condo." That had been another argument. Her mom had insisted she use the family's interior designer, but Andrea had stood her ground. And she was glad she had. She couldn't be happier with the result. Every square inch of the place reflected her personal touch.

"That's a shame. I hope you pick it back up again."

She shrugged. "It's been so many years since I touched a charcoal pencil, I probably wouldn't remember what to do with it."

"You had incredible talent. It would all come back with a little practice." He extended a hand toward the couch. "Have a seat. I'll share my cookies with you."

"Those are for you. I already ate too many."

She took a seat and he sat next to her, the sketches now behind them. She'd also done a self-portrait and given it to Bryce on his seventeenth birthday. That one wasn't displayed. She didn't expect it to be. Carla wouldn't have appreciated having to look at a sketch of her new boyfriend's ex every time she came over. Any girlfriends Bryce had had since probably wouldn't have, either.

The only one she could put a name or face to was Carla. Although her dad had kept her up to date on some of the people in Murphy, he'd been fairly tight-lipped about Bryce.

"You said someone recently put you through the wringer." As soon as the words left her mouth, she wished she could draw them back. Sure, they'd agreed to renew a friendship. But his love life was none of her business. If he shared his, he'd expect her to relay her own pathetic story. Before she could take back her comment, he spoke.

"Her name was Pam. We met through mutual friends. She'd moved here from Franklin to escape an abusive boyfriend."

She shook her head. "That's something I'll never understand. Both guys who hit women and women who put up with it."

"Sometimes they think they can't do any better, or the abuser convinces them they deserve it. Pam grew up in a really dysfunctional home. I was amazed she had it together as much as she did. But she still had lots of stuff to overcome. I thought she was doing pretty well."

"So how did it end?"

"He finished his jail time and she went back to him."

"Oh, no." The woman had to have been crazy to walk away from a kind, gentle man like Bryce.

"You guys could have been sisters."

His tone was soft, but the words had the same effect as a bucket of cold water being poured over her. Was that why he'd gotten involved, because Pam had reminded him of her?

A heavy silence hung between them, until Cooper approached to put a big paw in her lap.

"So now you're ready for that greeting." She gave it a couple of shakes.

For the next two hours, the conversation stayed light. Finally, she rose to leave.

Bryce stood also. "Give me a second to get his bed, and I'll walk you home."

He disappeared down the hall, then emerged a short time later, carrying a large fur-covered object.

"You think he'll be all right in my living room?"

He clipped on the dog's leash and moved toward the door. "He should be fine."

She hoped so. If he was in her room, she'd wake up every time he shifted positions. Over the past six months, she'd grown too accustomed to sleeping alone.

The dog loped along the trail in front of them, stopping twice to lift his leg. At least he was getting that out of the way.

Once inside, she took the bed from Bryce and dropped it against one wall. It was the end of the living room closest to the hall. She could have her privacy without Cooper feeling too isolated.

Bryce rested one hand on the doorknob. "If you have any problems, call or text me."

"I'm sure we'll do fine." She had no experience with dogs, or animals of any kind. But how hard could it be?

She locked the door behind him, then got ready for bed, allowing the dog to follow. When she'd finished putting on her pj's, she clapped her hands and stepped into the hall. "Okay, Cooper, time for bed."

His ears lifted, but he stayed where he was. Maybe she was supposed to whistle. That was going to be a problem.

"Cooper, come." She waved a hand, motioning him toward her. He crossed the room and joined her in the hall. After some more coaxing, he stepped into his bed, turned two full circles and plopped down with a thump.

"Good dog." She petted him a few times and turned off the living room lights. It was early enough, so she could spend some time reading.

She still hadn't decided how long she'd stay. After next week, she'd be down to five weeks of vacation. If she wanted to take some long weekends, she'd better not burn through all of it. Maybe three weeks. By then she'd be ready to head back.

As she slid between the crisp sheets, a sense of heaviness settled over her like a cloak. Tension crept across her shoulders, and her insides tightened. What was wrong with her?

She picked up her phone and touched the Kindle app. Reading before bed had been a longtime habit. It was the surest way to shut down her brain so she could get some quality sleep.

The last page she'd read came up, midway through the newest book by one of her favorite women's fiction authors. She fluffed the pillows behind her and settled in.

After reading a few pages, she lowered the phone and rolled her shoulders, but the heaviness wouldn't leave. She recognized this feeling. It was the same thing she always felt when facing something she dreaded. Like a lunch date with her mother. Now it was the thought of going back to Atlanta.

Well, she was just going to have to deal with it. Sure, her ex was there. But she wasn't the first woman to have her self-esteem trampled by a cheating husband. And she certainly wouldn't be the last.

Soon she'd go back home and continue doing what she'd been doing for the past six months—avoiding routes that would take her anywhere near his office or the home they'd shared. She was even avoiding the hospital when she could.

And that was what she'd continue doing until thoughts of Phil with his new girlfriend didn't conjure up any more emotion than a trip to the mailbox. In the meantime, she'd occupy every spare moment with work.

The heaviness increased, pressing down on her until her shoulders ached. Now that she'd decided to keep the Murphy place, she didn't want to go back to Atlanta. At all.

She didn't even want to return to her job. The realization stunned her.

What was wrong with her? She loved her job. It defined her and gave her life meaning.

It also consumed her.

Bryce's words rang through her mind. *Sometimes it's good to slow down.*

She didn't know how to slow down. When she was younger, her mother wouldn't let her. When she got older, she wouldn't let herself.

If she didn't go back to her job, what would she do?

An image flashed through her mind, her pregnant friend, face glowing with love for her expanding family. She wanted to sell her business and had insisted Andrea would be the perfect fit.

No, out of the question. She'd be crazy to give up a stable, high-paying job for the headaches of self-employment to earn a fraction of what she was currently making. Totally impractical. And as she'd told Bryce, she was all about practicality.

She pushed the thoughts aside and returned to reading

until her eyes grew heavy. Finally, she placed her phone on the nightstand and curled up on her side.

Her thoughts grew more random, that telltale sign that sleep wasn't far away. She drifted on the sea of nothingness, the tide drawing her further from consciousness. Until the click of toenails against the hardwood floor pulled her back.

She opened her eyes. Cooper stood in her doorway, half in and half out, black body silhouetted against the dim glow of the bathroom's night-light.

"Cooper, go lie down."

He emitted a soft whimper.

She tried the command again. It didn't work any better than it had the first time. She heaved a sigh. Bryce had warned her. Cooper was used to sleeping in his room. In a strange house, away from his master, she couldn't expect him to be content alone in the living room.

"Okay, Cooper. You win."

When she dropped his bed at the foot of hers, he immediately plopped down and curled up, head resting on his front paws. She crawled back into bed and resumed her favorite sleeping position.

Outside, the wind picked up, a faint, distant howl. She soon found herself again hovering at the precipice, ready to slide into unconsciousness.

Another sound began, much closer than the wind. It was soft and low-pitched, followed by silence. Then again, repeating in a steady rhythm.

She opened her eyes. *Great.* A snoring dog.

Something scraped across the bedroom window, and tension spiked through her. She willed herself to relax. It was only a tree branch. The house was securely locked— this time with newly installed dead bolts.

And Cooper was sleeping at the foot of her bed. His presence brought more security than she'd expected, and she was glad to have him there. Snoring and all.

Whether from the break-ins, the dead squirrel in her mailbox, the threatening note, the run-in with Matt or the visit from Drysdale, she wasn't sure.

But a sense of uneasiness had wrapped around her.

And it wouldn't let go.

SIX

An old Beatles tune played in the living room, making the old house feel much less lonely. Andrea placed a stack of sweaters in the open box on her bed. There was no need to keep them. She'd outgrown them years ago, along with the other items in the box.

The music faded, and the first strains of "Here Comes the Sun" drifted into the room. As soon as Bryce left after picking up Cooper, she'd looked for some happy music to serenade her while she cleaned and sorted. She had plenty to choose from. Her dad grew up in the sixties and early seventies and had an enviable collection of CDs at the Murphy house. The Beach Boys, the Rolling Stones, Elvis and numerous others had a permanent place on the Wheaton shelf.

At least at this Wheaton residence. Pop music had never found its way into the Atlanta house. Her mother wouldn't have stood for it. Anything not high-brow enough to be performed by the London Philharmonic was beneath her.

Andrea folded down the flaps of the box and sang along. The lyrics weren't deep, but they were fun. She'd always liked that era of music because her dad had. She liked her mom's symphony music, too. But there'd been something special about blaring the Beatles through the house, her and her dad singing at the top of their lungs.

She toted the box into the living room and set it on top of another one near the door. She now had every room back in order except the master bedroom.

The "get rid of" stack was smaller than she'd anticipated, partly because there wasn't that much clutter. After her grandparents had passed away, her dad had donated their clothing and personal items to the Humane Society thrift store. And since this wasn't her parents' primary residence, the majority of their personal possessions weren't here.

If her mother were the one tackling clearing out the house, it would be much barer. Andrea hadn't been that unemotional. Too many of the items had sentimental value. Throughout her childhood, the Murphy house had been her retreat, the special place she and her father shared. They'd built so many memories.

She picked up a chunk of quartz displayed on the bookcase. She'd found it during one of their trips to the Hiwassee Dam. That was the time her father had tried to teach her how to skip rocks. His would skate across the smooth surface, bouncing three or four times. Hers would land in the lake with a splash. She never did get the hang of it.

She laid the rose-colored stone back on the shelf. Her mother would look at it as a meaningless hunk of rock, occupying space that should belong to an engraved Humidor vase, or some other collectible. She and her father saw it as yet another opportunity to say, "Remember when…"

She picked up a spiral-bound notebook she'd put on

the desk earlier and slid it under a roll of duct tape in one of the drawers. As she pushed it closed, a longing stirred, the desire to create. She tried to shake it off, but it only intensified.

When she'd cleaned up her bedroom, she'd come across one of her old sketch pads and a box of charcoal pencils. At the time, they'd meant nothing. Now they called to her.

She pulled the items down from the closet shelf and carried them into the living room. After positioning herself on the couch, feet propped up on the coffee table, she glanced around the room. Two old bottles sat on the rolltop desk. When she and Bryce had found them on the property as children, they'd thought they'd found buried treasure. In spite of the age of the bottles, most of their value was sentimental.

She put the pencil to the paper and began to sketch with short, quick strokes. Silhouettes appeared, and the objects took shape, growing more three-dimensional as she layered in the shading.

A sharp rap sounded on the door. Her hand jerked, and a short, dark diagonal line cut into the drawing. Two other knocks followed the first. She thrust the pad aside and grabbed her phone from the coffee table. Eight o'clock. Bryce wouldn't be bringing Cooper over for another hour.

She took a deep breath and tried to slow her racing pulse. Intruders didn't knock. And it couldn't be a ploy to see if anyone was home. With the rental car sitting in the driveway and all the lights on inside, the house obviously wasn't vacant.

She crossed the room and peered around the edge of the drapes covering the front window. A man stood on her porch, turned partially away from her. It wasn't Bryce. Standing in profile, he looked an awful lot like... No, couldn't be.

She moved to the side to shout through the closed door. "Who is it?"

"Melvin Drysdale."

She'd been right. What did it take to get rid of the man? A restraining order? She shot off a text message to Bryce.

Drysdale here.

Then she leaned forward to shout through the door. "Didn't you get my message? I've decided not to sell."

"I got your message, but I think you'll want to re-consider."

"The property isn't for sale."

"Everything's for sale at the right price." He paused. "Will you please come outside so we don't have to shout through the door? Or open the window? You know I'm harmless."

Yeah, he looked harmless enough. But this was a conversation she didn't need to have.

He continued before she could respond. "I've got an offer in my hand. All you have to do is sign on the dotted line."

She hadn't had an appraisal done, but the figure he rattled off was easily 50 percent more than the market value.

"This home belonged to my family. You can't put a dollar amount on that."

"What would your father want? Would he want you saddled with a deteriorating property, more trouble than it's worth, or would he want you to take the money and enjoy yourself?"

Heat built in her chest. How dare he claim to know what her dad might have wanted? Before she could respond, another raised male voice reached her from somewhere outside.

"He'd want her to follow her heart, which means keeping the place she loves so much."

Andrea swung open the door in time to see Bryce climb the three steps onto her porch. A leash was wrapped around his right hand, the other end attached to Cooper's collar. He'd positioned himself between the dog and Drysdale, which was a good thing. Cooper stood at attention, eyes fixed on Drysdale, a low growl rumbling in his throat.

Bryce gave the man a stiff smile. "I'm sure there are other comparable properties for sale in the Murphy area. I'd suggest you go talk to a Realtor and see what's available, because this one isn't."

A chilly gust blew through the open door. Dried leaves danced across the yard, the rustle growing and then fading. A similar gust had probably allowed Bryce to approach without the other man hearing him.

Drysdale shifted his gaze between the dog and the pistol holstered at Bryce's hip and backed down the steps. His eyes met hers. "Hang on to my card, because you'll change your mind. You'll find this place just isn't worth it."

Bryce cocked a brow, his expression cool. "Is that a threat?"

"Just stating facts." Drysdale spun on one heel and stalked toward the Lexus waiting in the drive.

Andrea stepped back to allow Bryce and his dog to

enter. "That man's got a lot of nerve." She closed the door behind them. "I'm glad you got my text."

"No more missed texts. I've got a notification on there now that you can hear at the other end of the house." He unclipped the leash from Cooper's neck, then drew his brows together. "Didn't Drysdale get your message?"

"He got it. He just figured he'd try to sway me to change my mind."

"Why?" He gave Cooper a hand motion, and the dog settled at his feet. "The property's pretty. It's got acreage with a small creek running across the back." The same creek ran through his own property. "But that's not hard to find up here. So why is he so dead set on buying this one when it's not for sale?"

"I don't know."

"Maybe he's working with the men who broke into your house. They're determined to find something before you do. Now they believe Dennis buried it. The best way to guarantee that you don't find it would be to convince you to sell the property."

She frowned. "That's kind of extreme. It would have to be something really valuable."

"Or really incriminating. Maybe they have more to lose if their secret gets out than the cost of this property."

When she moved to the couch, the dog followed, plopping down at her feet.

Bryce took a seat next to her and picked up the sketch pad she'd left on the coffee table. "Did you do this today?"

"I was working on it when Drysdale showed up."

A smile of approval climbed up his cheeks. "Good. I'm glad to see you drawing again. You have too much talent to let it go to waste." He laid the pad back on the table. "Drysdale's out of Atlanta, right?"

"Marietta, which is a suburb of Atlanta."

He nodded slowly. "I'm going to run his name and see if anything shows up. Also, a friend I went to the academy with works for the Atlanta PD. I'll ask him to check to see if Drysdale is the subject of any investigations."

"I'd appreciate that. Something about the guy doesn't sit right with me."

"Me, neither. In fact, if you'll give me the names of your dad's business partners, I'll have him check those, too."

She nodded. "I'll write them down for you."

When Bryce walked out the door an hour later, he left with a handwritten list of names and no dog.

She knelt to cup Cooper's face in her hands. "I didn't think I'd say this, but I'm glad you're here."

Drysdale had made her uneasy from the first time she'd met him. Cooper's reaction had been even stronger. That deep growl hadn't stopped until Drysdale had gotten halfway to his car. If Bryce hadn't kept a firm grip on the leash, the dog might have taken a bite out of the man.

She rose, dread curling through her.

Animals often sensed the evil in people.

There was a reason Cooper didn't like Drysdale.

Bryce walked with Cooper along the trail leading to Andi's house. He held the leash but didn't have it connected to the dog's collar. It wasn't necessary. The dog wouldn't wander. If he did, one sharp command would bring him back.

He emerged from the trees right behind Cooper. It

was early afternoon, but he'd have to leave for his shift in thirty minutes, and he wanted to check on Andi.

She'd gotten back yesterday after a trip to Atlanta to sort through her dad's home office. According to Andi, when he'd gotten licensed for financial planning and gone into business with his two partners, he'd kept some of his CPA clients and handled their books from home. Over the two-day period, she'd notified all of them about her father's death and returned their records.

Her parents' personal paperwork, she'd brought with her in boxes. Eventually she'd have to go back to her job and condo. The odds of her moving to Murphy permanently were almost nil.

He stepped onto the porch and rapped on the door. There was a bell, but it had stopped working years ago. Dennis had done whatever work was necessary to keep the old house from deteriorating. A nonfunctioning doorbell didn't fall into the must-be-done category.

The door swung open, and Andi invited him inside. "Is it that time already?"

"Almost. How's the paperwork coming?"

"Pretty good." She bent to scratch Cooper's neck. She was apparently getting used to him. Maybe she was even starting to like him. She hadn't complained about having him there, anyway. Other than the snoring.

Of course, he'd spent only two nights with her so far. Five days had passed since Sunday's squirrel incident, but for three of them, she'd been in Atlanta. And he'd worried about her the entire time she'd been gone.

Now she was back, at least for a couple of weeks. During the hours he was at work, he was trusting her safety to Cooper, along with the alarm system Tri-State had installed yesterday. Now both doors and all the win-

dows had sensors. He'd have preferred a motion detec-
tor in the living and dining area, but if Cooper decided
to roam during the night, he'd set it off.

Andi moved into the dining room, where a chair was
pulled away from the table. A manila file folder lay at
that place, with several more stacked to the side. An open
box sat on the floor, about one-half full of files.

"I'm fortunate my dad was an accountant. He really
had his affairs in order. Since he added my name to everything, nothing will even need to go through probate.
Usually kids have it much harder than this."

She sat down and picked up the single file folder and
slid it into the box. "I found their life insurance policies.
Let's just say I won't have anything to worry about for
a long time. Of course, my dad's lawyer is working on
locating all the assets."

He nodded. When everything was said and done, Andi
was going to be a very wealthy lady. She'd always been
well-to-do, but the money had belonged to her parents.
Now it was all hers. Which put her even more out of his
league.

She pulled the next folder off the stack. "Oh, wow."

He looked over her shoulder at what she held. It was
labeled "Mercedes C300 Coupe."

"This was the car they died in." She ran a hand over
the folder, then opened it. The file contained maintenance records.

She picked up the top receipt. It was from the
Mercedes-Benz dealership in Atlanta. From where he
stood, he couldn't read what had been done.

For several moments, Andi read silently. When she
swiveled her head to look up at him, her jaw had gone lax.

"What is it?"

"Work the dealership did." She looked down at the receipt. "R and R brake pads, turn rotors, adjust calipers. This is dated November 2. Three weeks before the accident, my parents had the brakes redone."

She stood and started to pace. "My mom was driving. She always went a good five or ten under the speed limit. The road wasn't just familiar. She'd been on it so many times, she could just about drive it in her sleep. And tiredness didn't play into it, because she only made it about two miles from my aunt and uncle's place. Now I know there's no way the brakes failed."

She stopped her pacing to stand in front of him. "So how did she drive off the side of a mountain?"

"I don't know." Bryce's chest clenched. Was it possible someone tampered with the car? The brakes likely didn't fail…unless someone cut the lines. Or maybe Dennis and Margaret had a push from behind, the same as Andi had.

If someone killed Dennis to get his hands on something, he wouldn't hesitate to take out Andi for the same reason. If the motive was revenge, would the killer feel Andi deserved to die for Dennis's sins?

Andi closed the folder. "I've already contacted the investigators and asked them to look at the brakes." She frowned. "I don't know if they'll be able to tell anything, though. I saw pictures. The car didn't catch fire, but it was completely mangled."

"They have ways of finding out."

"My mom may have gotten distracted, even swerved to miss a deer. But in light of everything that's happened, I don't think that's the case."

He didn't, either, which made his concerns for Andi's safety even greater.

Cooper rose from his spot in the corner of the room and walked to the back door.

"You need to go out, buddy?"

The dog's tail wagged. Bryce picked up the leash and hooked it to his collar. Without it, the dog would still be sniffing underbrush and tree trunks fifteen minutes later. Something about the leash said business.

Bryce walked out the door behind Cooper, who headed for the nearest tree. When finished, the dog stood at attention, sniffing the air.

"What is it? Do you smell something?"

Bryce scanned the woods, straining to hear any sounds of movement over the rustle of the breeze through the trees. Was Matt snooping around again?

After listening for another minute, Bryce gave a tug on the leash. "Come on, boy. Let's go in." It was probably just an animal.

Bryce opened the back door and followed the dog inside, casting a final glance at the woods. There was movement in the distance, a flash of color. Cooper had been right. Someone was out there.

"I'll be back."

Andi looked at him, brows raised. He'd answer her questions later. He closed the door behind him, then bounded down the deck's stairs, through the small backyard and into the woods.

After reaching the area where he'd seen someone, he stopped and listened. Nothing. He scanned the woods, turning in a slow circle. Three quarters of the way around, his gaze locked onto a figure some distance away, running toward the Langman property. In fact, he'd probably reached it by now and was no longer in Andi's woods.

But that didn't matter. He had been. And he'd been warned.

Bryce charged after him, but he had too much of a head start. Matt would probably be inside the house by the time Bryce emerged from the woods. But that wasn't going to stop Bryce from confronting him.

He headed for the Langman porch. The same as before, Matt's old man answered the door. "What are you accusing my boy of this time?"

"Let me talk to him."

"He ain't here. Went to jail last night. Arrested for drunk and disorderly conduct."

"Did you bail him out?" He usually did. That was part of Matt's problem. His daddy never let him face the consequences of his actions.

"Nope. Gonna let him rot in there for a couple of days first. Boy needs to learn a lesson."

A couple of days wasn't going to provide the lesson Matt needed. But Langman wouldn't receive that truth from him. The old man didn't show the hatred toward him that he did toward the Wheatons, but ever since Bryce broke off his friendship with Matt, Langman had treated him with cold disdain.

Bryce turned to go, but Langman's voice stopped him. "So, what did he do?"

"Nothing."

He descended the porch steps, and the door closed behind him.

Matt had done nothing. He wasn't even there.

Or Langman was lying, covering for him.

Checking out his story would be easy enough. He'd just look at last night's arrest records. Or put Matt's name into an inmate search.

He sincerely hoped it wouldn't be there. Then he'd know for sure Langman was lying and it was only Matt prowling Andi's woods.

Matt held a lot of animosity toward her. If he never saw her again, he'd be happy. But Bryce didn't believe for a moment that he wanted her dead.

Maybe the guys who ransacked her house were connected with Matt. Or maybe they were working on their own.

It didn't matter.

Something told Bryce they played for keeps.

SEVEN

Andrea dragged a twelve-foot ladder from the shed. The thing weighed a ton. Rather than a stepladder, it was an old, straight wooden one and had lain against the wall as long as she could remember. It had probably belonged to her grandfather. Maybe even her great-grandfather.

Now that she'd decided to keep the place, all the projects her dad had let go over the years screamed at her. She could afford to hire contractors to whip everything into shape. In fact, she'd already gotten recommendations from Bryce for a plumber to change out the toilet that let water continually trickle into the bowl and an electrician to figure out why the breaker tripped every time she plugged something into the bathroom outlet.

But tackling some of the jobs herself gave her something to do. Slowing down didn't mean she had to sit idle.

Leaving the shed door open, she gripped a rung and dragged the ladder across the backyard. She'd left Bryce out front, trimming limbs that hung too low over the driveway. He was probably working on cleanup now. She hadn't heard the whine of the chain saw for a while.

Instead, music filled the air. She'd brought the CD player out to the deck and plugged it into an exterior outlet. This time it wasn't the Beatles' greatest hits. She'd inserted an Elvis Christmas CD.

The world wasn't going to cancel Christmas just because her life had fallen apart. She might as well quit fighting it. Maybe she'd even get a tree, do a little decorating.

If you can't beat 'em, join 'em.

One of the few idioms that had never come out of her mother's mouth. Andrea hadn't been allowed to swim downstream with the masses. Her mother had always pushed her to be better and work harder than everyone else. And she had.

Not that it had done her any good. No matter how hard she'd tried, she'd never quite met her mother's expectations.

She stopped next to the deck and dropped the ladder parallel to the house. Now that the chain saw had fallen silent, the music helped drown out the hum of male voices next door. Apparently Mr. Langman had left Matt in jail less than twenty-four hours before breaking down yesterday afternoon and bailing him out.

Now Matt was hanging out with his friends, probably drinking and puffing on something other than tobacco. Every so often, raucous laughter rose above the other sounds. They had a fire going in the fire pit, too. She'd been catching whiffs of smoke each time the wind shifted.

After moving to the other end of the ladder, she gripped the sides and lifted, struggling against the weight as she worked it toward an upright position. The sky was gray, and the early December air held a bite, but with the exertion of her activities, she'd stopped feeling it some time ago.

"What do you think you're doing?"

She started, almost dropping the ladder. When she looked over one shoulder, Bryce was hurrying toward her. She'd asked him the same question when she'd caught him cutting up her tree last Sunday.

"Cleaning out gutters." She tilted her head upward to where leaves overflowed the metal sides and trees had sprouted in the trough.

"You don't need to be working off the top of a ladder."

She ignored his admonition and continued what she'd been doing. She needed to either get the thing fully upright or drop it. Since she'd gotten this far, she was determined to finish.

Leaves crunched as Bryce stomped toward her. His arms circled her, hands gripping the sides of the ladder, and the weight got suddenly lighter. He didn't release it until he had it securely positioned.

"Those gutters are almost ten feet off the ground. I'll take care of them."

His voice was low, filled with determination. When she turned to face him, he stared her down with his stern gaze.

But that wasn't what unsettled her. It was how he stood so close, exuding competence and masculinity. His North Carolina Tar Heels jacket was zipped in the front, and day-old stubble covered his jaw. A couple of wood chips had gotten trapped in his windblown hair, and her fingers tingled with the urge to reach up and remove them. Twelve years and one cheating spouse later, how could that electricity still be there?

She stepped to the side to put a little distance between them, suddenly aware of her own disheveled appearance. She'd found a faded pair of blue jeans with grass stains on the knees and donned one of her dad's insulated flannel shirts, rolling the sleeves to a point just above her wrists. Her hair had been in a neat ponytail when she'd started, but after two hours of yard work, most of the sides had escaped the scrunchie and blew into her face with each breeze. But she wasn't out to win any beauty contests, or even impress any men.

She planted her hands on her hips. "You got away with cutting up the tree because you started it when I wasn't here. I'm not going to attempt a toilet replacement, but I think I'm talented enough to handle cleaning out gutters."

"It has nothing to do with talent or ability. You could get hurt."

"I can get hurt driving to the grocery store."

She stalked to the shed and rummaged through the items on one of the shelves until she found what she was looking for. There was probably something more suited for cleaning out gutters than a hand spade, but it was better than using her fingers, with or without the gloves she wore. She'd found them on another shelf, not sliding her hands into them until she'd thoroughly checked them for spiders.

When she emerged from the shed, Bryce was standing by the door, expression stormy. He followed her across the yard. "I'm happy to help with anything you need done. And if you insist on paying someone, I know several people who would jump at the chance to earn some extra money."

"I'm going to hire people for some projects. Just not everything." She climbed the ladder, spade handle stuffed into her back pocket. The rungs creaked with every step. She hesitated, adding *fiberglass stepladder* and *metal extension ladder* to her mental shopping list.

"FAST FIVE" READER SURVEY

Your participation entitles you to:
* ✳ 4 Thank-You Gifts Worth Over $20!

Complete the survey in minutes.

Get **2 FREE** Books

See inside for details.

Dear Reader,

Since you are a lover of our books, your opinions are important to us… and so is your time.

That's why we made sure your **"FAST FIVE" READER SURVEY** can be completed in just a few minutes. Your answers to the five questions will help us remain at the forefront of women's fiction.

And, as a thank-you for participating, we'd like to send you **4 FREE THANK-YOU GIFTS!**

Enjoy your gifts with our appreciation,

Pam Powers

To get your
4 FREE THANK-YOU GIFTS:

✳ Quickly complete the "Fast Five" Reader Survey
and return the insert.

"FAST FIVE" READER SURVEY

1 Do you sometimes read a book a second or third time? ○ Yes ○ No

2 Do you often choose reading over other forms of entertainment such as television? ○ Yes ○ No

3 When you were a child, did someone regularly read aloud to you? ○ Yes ○ No

4 Do you sometimes take a book with you when you travel outside the home? ○ Yes ○ No

5 In addition to books, do you regularly read newspapers and magazines? ○ Yes ○ No

YES! I have completed the above Reader Survey. Please send me my 4 FREE GIFTS (gifts worth over $20 retail). I understand that I am under no obligation to buy anything, as explained on the back of this card.

❏ I prefer the regular-print edition
153/353 IDL GM3W

❏ I prefer the larger-print edition
107/307 IDL GM3W

FIRST NAME	LAST NAME

ADDRESS

APT.#	CITY

STATE/PROV.	ZIP/POSTAL CODE

◀ If offer card is missing write to: Reader Service, P.O. Box 1341, Buffalo, NY 14240-8531 or visit www.ReaderService.com ▶

BUSINESS REPLY MAIL

FIRST-CLASS MAIL   PERMIT NO. 717   BUFFALO, NY

POSTAGE WILL BE PAID BY ADDRESSEE

READER SERVICE
PO BOX 1341
BUFFALO NY 14240-8571

NO POSTAGE
NECESSARY
IF MAILED
IN THE
UNITED STATES

"FAST FIVE" READER SURVEY

Your participation entitles you to:
✱ **4 Thank-You Gifts Worth Over $20!**

Complete the survey in minutes.

Get **2 FREE** Books

Your Thank-You Gifts include **2 FREE BOOKS** and **2 MYSTERY GIFTS**. There's no obligation to purchase anything!

See inside for details.

Dear Reader,

Since you are a lover of our books, your opinions are important to us... and so is your time.

That's why we made sure your **"FAST FIVE" READER SURVEY** can be completed in just a few minutes. Your answers to the five questions will help us remain at the forefront of women's fiction.

And, as a thank-you for participating, we'd like to send you **4 FREE THANK-YOU GIFTS!**

Enjoy your gifts with our appreciation,

Pam Powers

To get your
4 FREE THANK-YOU GIFTS:

✱ Quickly complete the "Fast Five" Reader Survey
and return the insert.

"FAST FIVE" READER SURVEY

1 Do you sometimes read a book a second or third time? ○ Yes ○ No

2 Do you often choose reading over other forms of entertainment such as television? ○ Yes ○ No

3 When you were a child, did someone regularly read aloud to you? ○ Yes ○ No

4 Do you sometimes take a book with you when you travel outside the home? ○ Yes ○ No

5 In addition to books, do you regularly read newspapers and magazines? ○ Yes ○ No

YES! I have completed the above Reader Survey. Please send me my 4 FREE GIFTS (gifts worth over $20 retail). I understand that I am under no obligation to buy anything, as explained on the back of this card.

❏ I prefer the regular-print edition
153/353 IDL GM3W

❏ I prefer the larger-print edition
107/307 IDL GM3W

FIRST NAME	LAST NAME

ADDRESS

APT.#	CITY

STATE/PROV.	ZIP/POSTAL CODE

She shook off the uneasiness. The ladder wasn't rotten. The sides and rungs looked strong and solid. It was the nature of the material. Rocking chairs, old houses—wooden things creaked.

Once satisfied with her position, she scooped out a spade full of decaying leaves and let them fall to the ground.

"Why are you insisting on doing this?"

She looked down at him. "Can't you see? I'm enjoying myself."

"Cleaning gutters." The doubt in his tone was reflected on his face.

"Yes."

Bryce had accused her of being a workaholic. Maybe she was. But that wasn't what this was about.

She loved the Murphy house because of what it had meant to her father. Giving it the attention it deserved made her feel close to him. The projects she'd tackled so far had been almost cathartic.

Especially the ones outside. She'd almost forgotten how much she used to love nature.

When she looked at Bryce again, he shrugged. "Suit yourself."

He walked to the shed and emerged with a rake. When he disappeared around the side of the house, she resumed her work. It was something they'd agreed on. She'd tackle outside projects only if he was home. Once he left for work, she'd remain locked in the house with Cooper, alarm set.

Hanging on to the aluminum gutter, she stretched to the right and flipped a final scoop of leaves over the edge. That was as far as she could safely reach.

Once on the ground, she wrestled the ladder over, an

inch or two at a time. When she'd finally gotten it positioned about three feet from where she'd started, she climbed it again, the creaks vibrating through the bottoms of her tennis shoes. She pulled the tool from her back pocket and stepped on the final rung.

It emitted the same unnerving creak. The crack of splitting wood registered a half second later and the step gave way.

A scream ripped a path up her throat. She released the spade and made a frantic grab for the side of the ladder, other hand still clutching the gutter.

The top of the ladder slid sideways, and she went with it, legs swinging in an attempt to find purchase. The gutter ripped through her gloved fingers as she fell, and she released the ladder, ready to try to break her fall.

Her right foot hit the ground first and turned inward with a snap. Pain shot through her ankle and up her leg, and she landed with a thud on her right hip. A second later, the ladder struck her shoulder, then fell across her left leg.

"Andi!" Panic laced Bryce's tone.

She looked across the yard to see him running toward her, expression a mix of concern and horror. He pulled the ladder off her leg and dropped to his knees next to her.

She shifted position and groaned. Her ankle and hip hurt. So did her shoulder and left calf where the ladder had struck her. Her right wrist, too. She'd apparently fallen on it when her ankle gave way.

Bryce put gentle hands on her shoulders. "Don't try to get up. I'm calling 911." He pulled his phone from his pocket.

She held up a hand. "Let me assess my injuries first. An ambulance might be a little overkill."

When she moved her foot, her ankle screamed in protest. Ice was definitely in order. She at least had a bad sprain, maybe even a break. She'd know more when she stood and put weight on it.

Her wrist was the same—a bad sprain. But she was sure nothing was broken. Some time in a brace, and she'd be good as new. The hip, shoulder and leg were probably just bruises.

"I think I'm okay." She lifted her hands, ready to allow Bryce to help her to her feet. Self-sufficiency wasn't going to benefit her at the moment.

After he'd helped her up, she gingerly tested the right ankle. She could put some weight on it as long as she kept the joint straight.

She limped to the deck, leaning on Bryce's arm, then sat on the steps. Movement in her peripheral vision drew her attention to the left.

Three figures watched from the tree line, Matt in the center. A guy she didn't recognize stood on Matt's left; Bradley Gunter was on his right. Bradley had always gotten into as much trouble as Matt. She'd never been sure who was the instigator. Maybe they both were.

When she glanced up at Bryce, she knew he'd seen them, too. He charged over to where the ladder lay on the ground.

She drew her brows together. "What are you doing?"

Instead of responding, he picked up one end. Two rungs were broken. She'd apparently taken out the second joint as she fell.

He turned the ladder, adjusting the angle. When he

looked up, his face was red and a vein throbbed in his temple.

But the anger wasn't directed at her. His gaze was fixed on Matt and his friends.

"Bryce?" What had he seen?

Ignoring her, he stalked past her toward the woods that separated the Langman and Wheaton properties. Both Bradley and Matt's other partner in crime spun and disappeared into the trees, kicking up dead leaves as they ran. Maybe they were smarter than she'd given them credit for.

Matt wasn't. Though his stance projected wariness, he was just cocky enough to stand his ground.

Bryce didn't stop until he stood toe to toe with Matt. When Bryce spoke, his words were too low to carry to the deck. He grabbed Matt by the shirt collar and yanked him forward. Andrea gasped.

"Bryce." She rose from the deck and took a step. Pain shot through her ankle. She needed a crutch or walking stick if she didn't want to risk further damage to the joint.

What had set Bryce off? Whatever it was, it wasn't worth getting into a physical altercation. She had no doubt who would come out on top. But that wasn't the point.

Matt struggled to break free of Bryce's grasp. "Let go of me."

Bryce ignored the plea. Andrea clutched the rail and watched him drag Matt across the yard. Matt's eyes were wide, every bit of cockiness gone. At six foot two, Bryce was a good four inches taller and probably outweighed Matt by fifty pounds. And Bryce was ticked.

Matt struggled some more, dragging his feet. "This is police brutality! I'm going to report you."

"Do you see a uniform? A badge? No, you don't. That means I'm not acting as law enforcement. Right now, I'm nothing but a concerned neighbor."

He gave him a hard shove, and Matt fell to his knees in front of the ladder.

"Andi could have been seriously hurt, maybe even killed."

Matt twisted his head around to look up at Bryce but didn't try to rise. "What are you talking about?"

"The ladder. You see these two broken rungs? Andi was standing on one of them when it gave way."

Andrea held up a hand. Bryce was overreacting, and he was going to get himself in trouble. "It's okay. This is what I get for using a ladder that was probably manufactured during the Civil War." She should have listened to him when he tried to stop her.

"Your fall was no accident. This ladder might be old, but there's not a bit of rotten wood on it." His gaze locked with hers, and something there sent a block of ice straight to her gut. "There are hacksaw cuts halfway through the top five rungs, right where they go into the side rails. He intended for this to happen, if not to you, to anyone who might help you out around this place."

The air whooshed out of Andrea's lungs, leaving her hollow inside. That could have been Bryce. Or any of the people he'd referred to who would jump at the chance to earn some extra money.

Matt rose and backed away, arms raised and eyes as wide as they'd been when Bryce dragged him across the yard. "Wait a minute. We heard her scream and came to see what was going on. You can't pin that one on me."

"That one?"

"Okay, I admit it. I put the dead squirrel in her box. I wrote the note, too. But I didn't do this. I swear. I ain't never tried to hurt nobody."

Bryce moved toward him. "If you don't want to be charged with attempted murder, I'd suggest you stay as far away from Andi and her property as humanly possible. If you're smart, you'll even avoid the whole right-hand side of your own."

Matt gave a slight dip of his head, then moved toward home at a good clip. After letting Bryce intimidate him, he wasn't demeaning himself further by running away. But he wasn't hanging around, either.

"I'm done for the day." Andrea started up the deck steps. "I need to ice my ankle, then wrap it."

The next moment, Bryce was beside her, sweeping her off her feet. She wrapped both arms around his neck and rested her head against his shoulder.

Her ankle was throbbing. But it was more than that. Over the past several months, her life had self-destructed. First her marriage. Then her parents. Now someone was trying to kill her.

And Bryce was there, offering her encouragement and support. They were friends. And friends went to bat for each other. But the fury he'd shown toward Matt and his fierce protectiveness toward her spoke of something deeper.

She tightened her hold, drawing from his warmth and strength. Right now, she needed him. She was hurting, both inside and out. The care he offered, whether as a friend or something more, she'd take.

Once inside, he gently laid her on the couch. "Are

you sure you don't need a doctor? I'll drive you to Murphy Medical."

"I'm positive." If she changed her mind, she'd let him take her. She still had the Accord, and would for a while longer. She'd gotten word yesterday—they were totaling her Escalade. There was too much damage to the frame.

Her mom's car still sat in the garage of their Atlanta home. It was one of those two-seater BMWs, classy and sporty at the same time. Andrea planned to sell it. She was more of an SUV kind of girl.

She pushed herself to an upright position. "Spending a couple hours in the emergency room doesn't sound like fun. If I'm not going to get anything accomplished, I'd rather do something I enjoy."

"Then let me get you some ice."

He disappeared into the kitchen and returned a couple of minutes later with a zippered plastic bag filled with ice and wrapped in a dish towel. After propping her foot up on a pillow he'd put on the coffee table, he tucked the pack around it. "How's that?"

"Cold."

"It's supposed to be." He sat next to her. "So what did you have in mind for something fun?"

"I was thinking about watching a movie." She'd brought back a TV with a built-in DVD player from her parents' house, determined to prove to Bryce that she was slowing down.

"Can Cooper and I join you? He loves movies. Especially ones with dogs. I rented *Hotel for Dogs*, and he was mesmerized."

"I haven't seen it." Actually, if a movie had been re-

leased anytime in the past ten years, she probably hadn't
seen it.

"If you want to watch it, I haven't returned it yet."

"You don't want to see it twice."

"I don't mind. Cooper will be thrilled."

She smiled. "We'd better keep Cooper happy if we
expect him to continue his guard-dog duties. Otherwise
he might go on strike."

"You have a point. I'll go get the movie. And the dog.
But first we need to file a police report."

"I was thinking the same thing."

While he called dispatch, she chewed her lower lip.
She was going to have to get a hasp and padlock for the
shed. Originally a one-room cabin, her great-grandparents
had lived there until the house was built sometime later.
The oldest building on the property, it hadn't locked securely in years. Her dad had never worried about it. No
one was going to steal a bunch of old tools.

Actually, no one had messed with the riding mower,
either. It had occupied its same spot in the corner forever,
until it finally gave up a few years ago. According to her
dad, Bryce had been keeping up the small portion of the
property that wasn't wooded ever since.

Bryce finished the call and pocketed his phone. "Do
you believe Matt?"

Her stomach tightened. That same question had circled through her mind for the past several minutes. "I
never thought I'd say this, but I do. When you said what
you'd found, he was as surprised as I was. I don't think
he's a good enough actor to fake that kind of shock."

"I was thinking the same thing." He put his arm
around her and pulled her against him. "I don't want to
let you out of my sight."

She closed her eyes, resisting the urge to lean into him. She shouldn't let him hold her this close. It was muddling her thinking.

Because right now, all she wanted was for him to hold her and never let her go. She needed to get a grip. If she didn't get her head back on straight, she was going to do something stupid.

She snuggled more tightly against him.

There'd be time for rational thinking later.

Tomorrow.

Bryce closed the door on a silent, empty house and jogged down the porch steps. Cooper was still at Andi's, already walked and fed. Bryce had taken care of that early this morning.

After law enforcement left last night, he'd come home for the dog and a handful of movies. He'd also brought over a frozen lasagna. It wasn't a home-cooked meal, but at least she hadn't had to make it herself.

They'd ended up watching two movies. At Andi's insistence, the second one had been an action-adventure flick. She'd said it was the least she could do after he'd sat through two viewings of *Hotel for Dogs*. He was pretty sure she'd enjoyed the testosterone-charged show as much as he had.

Actually, he'd enjoyed both. He'd sat on the couch next to her, his arm around her, Cooper at their feet. Maybe that wasn't how "just friends" did movies. But having Andi snuggled against his side had seemed so natural. Maybe it was because of the many times they'd done just that. Not there. They'd never had a TV at the house growing up. But he and Andi had watched their fair share of movies cuddled together at the old Henn Theater downtown. All these years later, it still felt right.

He stepped onto her porch and rapped on the door. This morning he was taking her to church, but not to either of the two she'd suggested. Colton and Tanner had invited him to theirs numerous times, and he'd always offered excuses. Now that he'd decided to go, he'd be in trouble with his friends if he went somewhere else. They'd all occupy an entire row at MountainView Community Church.

Andi opened the door and waited for him to enter. She had her weight shifted to one foot, a crutch under each arm.

He frowned. "Are you sure you're up for this?"

"Positive. I'm pretty good at maneuvering on these things." To prove her point, she made her way into the dining area and back again. She still hadn't gone to the doctor. Fortunately, Colton's wife, Mandy, had the crutches tucked away in a closet, souvenirs from an ACL tear she'd suffered as a high school cheerleader.

A few minutes later, a horn beeped. When they walked out the door, Tanner was sitting behind the wheel of his Silverado, and his fiancée, Paige, was climbing out the passenger side.

She held up a hand in greeting. "Us girls will sit in the back. You guys take the front. A lot more leg room."

Bryce approached them and made introductions. Other than the brief meeting the night they'd caught Matt prowling in the woods, Andi didn't know Tanner. And she hadn't yet met Paige.

After helping Andi into the truck, he took a seat up front. Soon the women were engaged in conversation behind him. They seemed to hit it off well, which was good. Andi liking his friends was important to him. If she was going to be spending time at the old house, he planned to include her in their get-togethers.

When they arrived at MountainView, they met Colton and Mandy just inside the door. There were more introductions, and by the time they took their seats near the front, the service was beginning. After a welcome and opening prayer, the worship band struck their first notes and song lyrics appeared on a screen over the drummer's head.

Several of the songs were modernized versions of familiar Christmas carols, and Bryce sang along softly. Andi stood next to him, smiling as she belted out the words. She'd always had a pretty voice. He didn't.

When the song service ended, the pastor took the podium. His message had a Christmas theme. The second week in December, Bryce had expected as much. He knew the Christmas story. Attending church at least once during the season had been a tradition in his family.

The pastor began his message talking about Jesus being Emmanuel—God with us. That wasn't a new concept for Bryce, either. He cast a sideways glance at Andi. She was leaning forward, wearing a gentle half smile. Since she was newly divorced and having just lost her parents, the thought of not being alone would probably resonate with her.

The next scripture named Jesus as Savior. As the preacher expanded on the point, Bryce frowned. It wasn't the first time he'd heard Jesus referred to as Savior. But now something about the thought disturbed him. Jesus being sent as a Savior implied that mankind needed saving.

When he pulled his attention back to the pastor, the

man was reading from First Timothy, a statement made by the Apostle Paul—"Jesus Christ came into the world to save sinners, of whom I am chief."

What? The man wrote over half of the New Testament, and he thought he was the worst sinner who ever lived?

When they stepped out into the sunshine some time later, Andi smiled up at him. "I'm glad we came." Her features held a serenity that he hadn't noticed before. He hoped she'd found peace inside those walls.

He'd found the opposite.

As he walked toward Tanner's truck, one statement circled through his mind, spoken by the pastor near the end of his message—"Without Christmas, there's no Easter, and without Easter, there's no salvation."

He'd always considered himself a pretty good person, at least since Dennis Wheaton pulled him onto the right path. He figured when he got to the gate, Peter would consult the book, see all his good deeds and let him in.

But maybe he had it wrong. What if he wasn't good enough? If the Apostle Paul needed saving, what did that say about him?

He climbed into Tanner's truck and fastened the seat belt. Now that church was over, they were all heading over to Colton and Mandy's house, where a large Crock-Pot full of roast, potatoes and carrots waited. An afternoon spent with his closest friends, talking and laughing, was just what he needed.

Since Andi arrived back in Murphy, hardly a moment had gone by that he hadn't worried over her safety. This afternoon he'd lay it aside. With her tucked away in Colton's house, surrounded by people, he could finally let down his guard.

As far as the uneasiness he'd left church with, he would set that aside, too. He'd have plenty of opportunity to delve into it more deeply later. Judging from Andi's reaction to the service today, she'd likely be making church attendance a regular part of her life.

And as long as she was in Murphy, whatever was a regular part of Andi's life would also be a regular part of his.

EIGHT

Bryce sat at the computer, nursing a cup of coffee and checking out world events. He had cable and often listened to the news if he was home for it, but keeping himself updated this way was more efficient. He could scan headlines and click on only the things that interested him.

His phone lit up next to the laptop, and he cringed. As soon as Andi was out of danger, he was going back to his old notification. What he had on there now sounded like Alvin and the Chipmunks trying to wake the dead.

It was serving its purpose, though. He hadn't missed a text since he set up the new alert.

He picked up the phone, and his pulse kicked up several notches. It was from Andi. You up?

He released a pent-up breath. Not a someone's-trying-to-kill-me text. He responded. For a while.

Have you had breakfast?

Hmm, if she wanted to cook for him, he certainly wouldn't complain. No.

On my way with Cooper.

Oh, no, not alone. He jumped up from the table and grabbed the jacket hanging on a hook beside the door. He shrugged into it as he descended the porch steps. A fine layer of frost covered the ground, and a chilly wind cut right through him.

Leaves crunched under his feet as he made his way toward the trail, the cold seeping through his socks. Maybe he should have slipped into some shoes, too. No, he'd deal with frozen feet before he'd let Andi walk over alone.

Up ahead, a door shut. He emerged from the woods in time to see Andi descend the steps, a foil-covered plate in one hand and a walking stick in the other.

She'd made a lot of progress with her ankle over the past four days. She still kept it wrapped and used a stick when on uneven ground, but the limp was almost gone. She'd said her wrist was doing fine, too, as long as she didn't bend it too far. The bruise on her leg had turned an angry blue-black. She'd lifted her pant leg and showed it to him, claiming she had a matching one on her shoulder and an even larger one on her hip.

As she made her way toward him, Cooper trotted along in front of her. Bryce knew the instant the dog saw him. Cooper bounded toward him, ears bouncing. Seconds later, large paws slammed into his chest.

"No, boy. Down." He lowered the dog to the ground, laughing. "We're still working on some things."

"He's excited to see you. He'll be glad when he's not stuck babysitting me anymore."

He took the plate she held and followed Cooper back down the trail. "Actually, he does the same thing when we're headed over here. I'm almost afraid he's going to choose you over me."

"I don't think you have anything to worry about."

She paused. "Why are you barefoot? It's thirty degrees out here."

"I'm not barefoot. I'm wearing socks."

"Which are probably frozen to the bottoms of your feet."

He frowned. "You might be right. I didn't take time to get my shoes. I don't like you stepping out the door alone."

"That's why I texted you. But I figured you'd wait at your front door for me. I'm easily in shouting range of you."

Yeah, but shouting range wasn't good enough. He wanted to keep her in visual range, too.

He swung open the door, then tilted his head toward the plate. A mouthwatering aroma was seeping around the foil. "What's in here?"

"It's called a giant pancake." She stood her walking stick by the door and followed him inside. "Super easy. You mix up the ingredients, then bake it in a cast-iron skillet. Slather melted butter over it when it's finished, sprinkle with sugar, and voilà, breakfast."

He placed the plate on the dining room table, and she sank into a chair.

"When my dad and I would come up here, mornings always included giant pancakes." She gave him a wistful smile. "We never had them at home. I think it was just something special for the two of us here."

He took two glasses from the cabinet. "I assume giant pancakes go good with orange juice."

She grinned. "Giant pancakes go good with everything."

After setting the table, he plopped a can of dog food into a bowl and put it on the floor. If Cooper didn't eat first, he'd stare at them with soulful eyes throughout their entire meal.

"One more thing. Dry socks. I can no longer feel my toes."

When he walked back into the room, Andi removed the foil from the plate to reveal eight pie-shaped pieces, already cut.

"You won't let me pay you for the work you're doing, but I figured you wouldn't turn down breakfast."

"No payment necessary. Your dad was more like a father to me than my own. I've always been happy to help out." He flashed her a teasing smile. "But I never turn down food."

He took a seat, then pulled two pieces of pancake onto his plate. "I got a call from my buddy in Atlanta during my shift last night."

"Anything interesting?"

"John Lassiter has a thing for driving fast. He averages a speeding ticket every quarter. He's a few points away from losing his license. Mark Barrand is in a lawsuit with the IRS. There's apparently some dispute over back taxes."

"And Melvin Drysdale?"

"He's been married several times. His last wife disappeared. He was a person of interest, but they never could prove his involvement. They still haven't found her."

"He probably hid her body under the floorboards so he doesn't have to share his wealth with her."

That scenario wouldn't surprise him. He stabbed his next bite. She'd asked him to check out her dad's partners and Drysdale. He'd done more. "I had him run your dad's name, too."

Her fork stopped halfway to her mouth, and her eyes met his.

"Nothing. He's completely clean."

Her shoulders dropped as she released a breath she'd apparently been holding.

"I hope you don't mind that I had him checked out."

"Under the circumstances, that was the smart thing to do." She heaved a sigh. "You know, this was my dad's favorite time of the year. My mom always had professional decorators come in and deck out the Atlanta house for Christmas. I think she was competing for the most spectacular house on the block."

She gave him another wistful smile. "We had so much fun doing it ourselves here—going to town, picking out the tree, loading it on a blanket on top of my dad's car. If we had ever damaged the paint, my mom would've killed us both."

He returned her smile. He'd been part of those preparations more than once. He and Andi had always spent the actual holiday with their respective families, but they'd made some great memories during those three or four weekends leading up to Christmas.

She fixed her eyes on the picture hanging on the wall opposite from where she sat. It was her own sketch, a scene from inside the Wheaton living room next door. A decorated Douglas fir stood in the corner, next to the fireplace. A fire burned inside, and stockings lined the mantel, names written in cursive. One said "Andi," one said "Dad" and one said "Bryce." A dog was curled up on the hearth. It wasn't part of the original scene. Andi had added it in memory of the black Lab Bryce had lost then.

When Andi met his gaze, her eyes sparkled with anticipation. "I want to get a tree and decorate the house for Christmas, the same as Dad and I used to do. I've just got to figure out how to get it here. Throwing it on top of the rental car is probably not a good idea."

"We can use the Sorento. I'll even take you today. We have plenty of time before I have to head in to work."

She finished her juice, then stood to take their empty dishes to the sink. "I've got some things I'm working on at the house. Can you pick me up in two hours?"

"Sure. Cooper and I will walk you home. With shoes, this time."

He slipped his feet into the tennis shoes he'd left in front of his recliner last night. When he opened the door, Cooper stood at attention, waiting for the command.

"Come on, you can go."

The dog darted outside and down the porch steps. Andi retrieved her walking stick and followed, and Bryce brought up the rear.

Cooper headed straight for the trail. He'd traveled the route enough that he knew the way. The dog had almost reached the corner of the house when he suddenly stopped. His ears lifted, and muscles rippled beneath his black coat.

Bryce rushed forward, tension spiking through him. "Cooper, stay."

Before he could grab the dog's collar, Cooper bolted away, charging into the backyard, toward the woods. Bryce gave a second and third command. Cooper ignored those, too, his barks echoing as he ran.

Andi held up a hand. "I'll make it the rest of the way. Go find your dog."

"Lock yourself inside. I've got to get my weapon." No way was he charging into the woods unarmed.

As soon as Andi had locked the door, he sprinted back to his house. When he emerged, Cooper was still barking. As near as he could tell, the dog had stopped somewhere near the back of Andi's property. Did he have Matt cornered?

Or someone else?

Bryce crept deeper into the woods, the weight of the pistol reassuring. Maybe he should call for backup.

And risk bringing units out for nothing more serious than an animal or a snooping neighbor. No, he needed to check it out.

As he skidded down the steep incline toward the creek, the barking grew louder. Ahead, black stood out against the browns and greens of nature.

When Bryce reached him, Cooper was at the base of a pine tree, looking up. Bryce shook his head. Just what he'd suspected. The dog had cornered a raccoon.

He pulled the leash from his pocket and clipped it to Cooper's collar. "Come on, goofball. Leave it alone."

With a tug on the leash, Bryce turned to head back up. To the right, a shallow cavern had been gouged from the side of the steep slope. That was the place where gold had been mined on the property.

The deepest part had long since been filled in. According to Dennis, it had happened when Andi's great-grandfather brought operations to a halt after a freak accident claimed one man's life. As kids, he and Andi would climb down the jagged slope and pretend they were old-time gold prospectors. He hadn't been there in years.

But someone had.

He clambered down to the bottom of the grade. The area that Andi's great-grandfather had filled so long ago was now dug out, with shovel and pickax marks left behind. A five-gallon bucket was tucked into the back of the hollowed-out area, two sluice pans dropped inside. Had Dennis known about the recent activity there? Probably not.

Bryce looked around him, searching for a hint as to where someone had entered and exited the property. The creek was only about fifteen feet away. During the spring thaw, it would grow to a width of two or three feet. Now it was little more than a trickle.

He scanned the opposite slope. He'd never met the owners of the property to their rear. But they likely weren't the ones tampering with the old mine. He'd already caught Matt on the property once.

Bryce marched through the woods, still holding Cooper's leash. When he stepped into the Langman backyard, Matt and the same two friends he'd been with Saturday were sitting around the fire pit. Smoke rose between them. But what wafted to him on the light breeze smelled sweeter than burning pine logs.

He stopped to stand between Matt and Bradley, who passed the rolled cigarette he'd been holding to the third guy. Cooper stood watching, curious but not aggressive in the slightest.

Bryce leveled his gaze on the stranger, who looked to be in his early twenties. "You new to Murphy?"

"Yeah. Moved here three weeks ago."

"Where to?"

"Up on Panther Top." He tilted his head toward where Ranger Road ended farther up the mountain.

"You live with your parents?"

He lifted his chin. "Just till I get my own place."

"Where'd you move from?"

"Tampa."

Bryce nodded. This wasn't the first time he'd seen it—parents take the kids out of the city and move them to a quaint mountain town with almost no crime. Then they hook up with the Matts of the community.

"I'm Bryce Caldwell. Live two doors down."

"Danny Carlson."

"Nice to meet you, Danny. Tractor Supply's looking for help. So are several other businesses around town. Getting a job will be good for you. Help keep you out of trouble."

Matt took the cigarette from his new friend. After hauling in a long drag, he held it for several moments, then blew it out slowly. "If you came over here to harass me and my friends, you can go ahead and leave."

Bryce shrugged. "Just getting acquainted."

He looked at the other two. If there was still gold on Andi's property, it was probably better to keep that fact quiet. Of course, knowing Matt, he'd probably already blabbed it.

Bryce leveled his gaze on him. "I'm curious about something. What'd you find in the old mine next door?"

"I don't know what you're taking about."

"I can tell you've been digging."

"Wasn't me."

"Come on, no one else knows it's back there."

Matt took one last drag, removed the end from the clip and tossed it into the fire. "So what if it *was* me? After what Old Man Wheaton did to my great-grandfather, I'm entitled to some of the Wheaton fortune."

It wasn't an admission, but it was the closest he was going to get. "I was just wondering if there was anything left or if they got it all out way back when."

Matt shifted his gaze to the fire. "Nah, nothing there. It's a dead mine."

"That's too bad."

Bryce lifted a hand in farewell and headed back into the woods. When he reached Andi's deck, she opened the door before he could knock. She'd apparently been watching for them.

"You got him." She heaved a sigh of relief and sank into a chair at the table. "I was afraid he was going to keep on going. There are hundreds of acres of woods out here." She paused. "Did you find anybody?"

"Yes and no. Cooper had run almost to the creek. You remember the old gold mine?"

Her eyes sparked with interest. "Yeah?"

"Matt has dug out a lot of what your great-grandfather filled in. He's been coming onto your property and panning for gold for who knows how long."

"He admitted it?"

"In so many words."

She lifted a brow. "Has he found anything?"

"He said no. But I'm pretty good at knowing when people are lying."

She nodded slowly, brain working behind her blue eyes. "No wonder he doesn't want me here. But it's stupid for him to try to run me off. If someone else owned the property, Matt wouldn't be any more welcome here than he is now."

"Maybe he isn't trying to scare you into selling. Maybe he just wants you to stay in Atlanta, the same as your father's been doing."

"Then the place would be vacant and he could come here whenever he wanted without getting caught."

Bryce sat opposite her, and she rested her chin in her hand.

"I wonder if that's what my dad hid, a large gold nugget."

"How would anyone know?"

"Maybe someone overheard him inquiring about its value."

He picked up a pen from the table and tapped it against the oak surface. "So let's say there's a rich vein of gold there. Your great-grandfather dynamited the opening of the mine, figuring no amount of gold was worth a man's life. For decades, it sat there untouched."

"Until Matt."

He nodded. "Your dad caught Matt snooping around and went to investigate. When he discovered Matt had reopened the mine, he figured he'd have some fun himself."

"My dad loved the outdoors. And he enjoyed trying new things. I could totally see him doing something like that." She pursed her lips. "But why wouldn't he have told me?"

"How much time did you spend alone with him in recent months?"

"Not as much as I should have." Her gaze dipped to her hands, which were clasped on the table.

He covered them with one of his. "You were both busy. My point is, he probably wouldn't have said anything in front of your mom, knowing how she felt about the property. And maybe at first he didn't realize just how much gold he was sitting on."

She pulled her hands free, straightening her shoulders. "And once he did, that's when he called you to set up a time to talk." She sat back in the chair, a smile climbing up her cheeks. "I knew it had to be something like this. I couldn't believe my dad would ever get involved in something illegal."

The grief and tension that had hung over her for the past two weeks had lifted, and the enthusiasm she projected was contagious. But clearing Dennis of wrongdoing didn't remove the danger.

"We still haven't ruled out foul play in your parents' accident. Or figured out how Drysdale plays into all this."

She pursed her lips. "Maybe he learned about the gold from Matt. I could see Matt bragging about some huge gold nugget he supposedly panned from my great-grandfather's abandoned mine."

"Does Drysdale seem like the type of person who'd run in the same circles as Matt?"

"He wouldn't have to. He could have been in hearing range when Matt was talking about it. Or maybe not Drysdale himself. Maybe somebody who knew somebody who knew Drysdale. You know, six degrees of separation."

He nodded. It was possible. Maybe Dennis Wheaton had been sitting on a small fortune and Drysdale had somehow gotten wind of it.

If that was the case, had Drysdale tried to convince Dennis to sell, then had him killed when he refused? The plan would have been almost foolproof. The only heir lived in Atlanta and hadn't stepped foot on the property in over a decade.

But Andi hadn't followed the plan.

And now she was the only thing standing between Drysdale and the property he was so determined to get.

It was a position that could prove to be deadly.

* * *

Andrea rose from the table and snagged her purse. "Let's go get that Christmas tree."

Bryce stood, too. "From the Rotary Club?"

"Yeah. Then we can hit Walmart. I'd like to use the same decorations, for old times' sake. But I'd rather start with new lights."

Bryce opened the door for her, then reached around to twist the lock. "Remember those old light strands where if one bulb burned out, half the strand went dark?"

She groaned. "How could I forget? I was always the one that had to dig through the branches and find the dead bulb without destroying the decorations."

After locking the dead bolt with the key, she grabbed her walking stick and let Bryce help her down the steps. Walking around the house wasn't bad. Maneuvering steps and trekking across unlevel ground was still a challenge.

"Mind if he goes with us?" Bryce tilted his head toward Cooper. "He loves car rides."

"What dog doesn't?"

As she climbed into the Sorento's passenger seat, she stifled a smile. Christmas tree shopping with Bryce. It wasn't what she'd envisioned when she first arrived in Murphy two weeks ago. But a lot had happened over the past two weeks that she hadn't envisioned.

Certainly not the unexpected sense of peace she'd found here. Or even that she and Bryce would be well on their way to forming an amicable friendship. It would never go any further than that, which was fine. That wasn't what she wanted. But she was glad to have her old friend back.

When they pulled into the lot fifteen minutes later,

Cooper stood in the back seat. Bryce stepped out of the truck and held up a hand. "Sit."

The dog complied, and Andrea closed the passenger door. "I'll make this quick. I know you've got work this afternoon."

"We've got plenty of time. I'll even be able to help you set up the tree and start decorating."

That was going to bring back some memories. She and her dad would always drive up the morning after Thanksgiving and buy a tree. Then they'd spend Friday afternoon and evening decorating. Most years, Bryce had been there, too, adding his own touches. The year they were both thirteen, they'd sat side by side on the couch, stringing popcorn. For every piece they strung, they ate two. It took them an hour to get a two-foot section completed.

They pulled from the lot a short time later with a Christmas tree tied to the roof. The Walmart stop didn't just yield lights. She also threw in a couple of Christmas CDs. One could listen to Elvis only so many times.

Bryce turned onto the four-lane, headed for home. "Are you going to decorate your condo, too?"

"No need. Christmas is less than two weeks away. I'll be here at least that long." She sighed. "Then my break will be over."

"You don't sound pleased."

"I love my job. The pay's good. I work with great people. But my stomach ties itself in knots every time I think about going back."

"Then don't."

"I can't just quit."

"People do it all the time."

She gave a wry laugh. "Not responsible, practical people."

"Sometimes you have to go out on a limb, take the plunge."

"I've never quit a job without having another, even better one lined up."

He cast her a sideways glance. "I bet you wouldn't starve before you found something else."

"That's beside the point. I could never bring myself to give up a good-paying job without something to step into. I'm too practical."

But maybe she did have something to step into. Maybe that chance run-in at Ingles wasn't coincidental after all.

Her pulse picked up speed, and her stomach fluttered with the same sense of anticipation she always got at the prospect of a new challenge.

A fresh start. A new life. It wasn't practical. But it was exactly what she needed.

She removed her phone from her purse.

"Who are you calling?"

"Angie Stanger. I ran into her at Ingles the other day. She's selling her store and decorating business, and I'm going to buy it."

He cocked a brow. "When you said you usually don't have a problem making decisions, you weren't kidding."

She smiled. "When I know what I want, I act immediately."

And this was what she wanted. It made absolutely no sense, but it felt 100 percent right.

Every job she'd ever had, her mother's connections had gotten her foot in the door. And her mother had never let her forget it. It didn't matter that she'd worked harder and longer than anybody else. According to her mother, she wasn't responsible for any of her own success.

Andrea pressed the Google icon and tapped the microphone. "Designs by Angie." The business name displayed, and she touched the screen. In a short time, she'd be saying "Designs by Andi." Or maybe she'd choose a different name altogether.

Excitement warred with trepidation. She'd never run her own business before. Hopefully the MBA would help. But no matter how much book knowledge she had, some lessons she'd have to learn by trial and error.

One thing was sure: this venture was completely her own. Whether she failed or succeeded, she'd have no one to blame or credit except herself.

Angie answered the call, her tone cheery and professional at the same time. Soon the professionalism fell away and she released a happy squeal.

Andrea smiled, Angie's excitement fueling her own. In career decisions, there were more things to consider than pay level and benefits. Sometimes the least tangible aspects were the most important—things like job satisfaction and doing what one loved. Having control of the job rather than the other way around.

Andrea finished the call and smiled over at Bryce. "I'm going next Monday to check out the store, look at the books and so on."

Five more days. She'd have scheduled it earlier if Angie wasn't overwhelmed with a huge decorating job in Chattanooga. If the meeting went like she expected it to, she'd be giving two-week notice to her employer as soon as she got home. Maybe even from Angie's parking lot.

Meanwhile, she'd use the next five days of downtime to work on the house. If the store and decorating business were a step down from her current management position, the old Murphy house was a leap away from the elegance of her condo. But it didn't matter. She'd always loved the old house, even in its semi-run-down condition.

Bryce pulled up next to the Accord. "Cooper can wait here a few minutes while we haul the tree in."

"Good plan." They'd get the tree inside, then bring the dog in on the leash. When Bryce was gone, she never let Cooper run free. She hadn't felt confident enough in her ability to control him. After this morning's wild chase, she probably never would.

She helped Bryce wrestle the tree off the roof, then wrapped her arms around the top while he grabbed the trunk.

"You sure you can carry that with your bad ankle?"

She cast a glance over one shoulder. "I'm fine as long as you don't make me walk backward."

Soon the tree was lying on the floor in front of the fireplace, and Cooper had curled up against the opposite wall. The two bags of lights waited on the couch.

While Bryce went to the shed to look for a hacksaw, Andrea retrieved the tree stand and boxes of decorations from the middle bedroom closet.

Tedious chores occupied the next fifteen minutes—rearranging furniture to make room in front of the window, trimming the trunk and getting the tree secured in the stand.

"Now the lights." She held up a hand. "Wait, I almost forgot." She walked to the master bedroom, still favoring her right ankle, and returned with the CD player. She'd carried it back there earlier when she'd worked on the bedroom. Soon the first strains of "Sleigh Ride" filled the room.

Bryce lifted a brow. "We're not going to listen to one of the new ones?"

"We can't do the tree without Elvis. It's tradition."

She handed him a box of lights, then set to work removing a second strand from its package. The CD was almost finished by the time they placed the last strand.

Bryce stepped back. "I can't believe we actually got six hundred lights on a six-and-a-half-foot tree. If you open the drapes, you could light up your whole front yard."

She gave him a playful punch. "Maybe it *is* a little extreme."

But she and her dad had always gone overkill on the lights. The ornaments, too. Her dad had said the overabundance of decorations made the tree look cheery. If there was any Christmas she'd need cheery, this was it.

Bryce glanced at the clock. "Unless I'm going to work dressed like this, I'd better head for home."

"Thanks for all your help. Now that the lights are strung, the rest of it is all fun stuff."

"I still hate to bail on you."

She shrugged. "I'm used to decorating alone. Phil never helped."

"Your ex?"

"Yeah." The first few years she'd decorated a nine-foot-tall artificial tree alone. The last few she hadn't even bothered. When Phil had been in medical school, his hours had been long. In residency, they'd been even longer.

"What happened?" He paused. "If you'd rather not say, I understand."

She crossed her arms. She really *would* rather not say. Telling the story involved admitting she hadn't been able

to hold on to her husband. As if she was somehow defi-
cient. But Bryce had told her about Pam. That was what
friends did, shared their hurts.

She drew in a stabilizing breath. "He's a neurosurgeon.
I worked my tail off putting him through medical school,
then supported us while he did his residency. I knew
someday it would be worth it. He'd have a great-paying
job, and we'd reap the rewards of all that sacrifice."

"And?"

"Nine months ago, he joined a successful neurosurgery
group. Six months ago, I came home from work early to
find him with our next-door neighbor."

"Oh, man. That stinks. I'm sorry."

"Thanks. I'm getting over it." Or maybe she wasn't.
Otherwise, she wouldn't still feel like throwing up every
time she thought about it.

He moved toward the door. "Is it okay if I stop by after
my shift? It'll probably be a little late."

"Sure. I might be in my flannel pj's."

"The acrobatic cats."

"You noticed."

She closed the door behind him and threw the dead
bolt. As she removed decorations from the first box, the
CD ended and the house fell silent.

She took a second one from its case, another Elvis
Christmas album, and swapped it with the first. Mo-
ments later, music swelled. But the house still felt empty.
She willed back some of the holiday spirit she'd felt with
Bryce at her side and pulled garland from a box.

That one holiday, they'd proudly displayed the stubby
popcorn garland front and center. It hadn't made it to a
second Christmas. The braided ribbon garland had survived the years. So had the pom-pom-and-soda-straw

garland. Half the fun of trimming the tree had been making new decorations to add to the eclectic collection they pulled out of the closet every year.

Once she had the garlands arranged, she started on the ornaments. She was trying. Really hard. She was decorating, and she'd do some baking—iced sugar cookies in the shapes of bells, trees, candy canes and snowmen. Maybe she'd even attend MountainView's Christmas Eve service.

MountainView was a little larger than the church she'd attended with Bryce and her father, but not by much. This past Sunday, sitting a few rows from the front with Bryce next to her, had brought back memories. Except this time it was different. She had a mission. She'd gone searching for something. She couldn't say she'd fully found it, but she was on her way. The future services she planned to attend would help. So would the Bible that currently lay open on her bedside stand.

She pulled another ornament from the box and folded back the tissue. A jolt hit her, shooting all the way to her toes.

It was a wallet-size family photo in an oval frame that she'd decorated with ribbon and paint and glitter. She'd been about ten.

She inserted a hook into the loop and hung it from one of the branches. Though she'd known it, the reality hit her full force. While Phil was bringing his new girlfriend to his family's Christmas gathering, she'd be spending her first holiday without her parents.

She sank onto the couch, despair settling over her.

A sense of loneliness that even Elvis's rich voice couldn't dispel.

NINE

Bryce walked through the woods, the flashlight beam illuminating the trail in front of him. He'd parked the cruiser in his driveway, then headed right over.

It would be fun to see what Andi had done with the place and reminisce over decorations he hadn't seen in more than twelve years. Although Dennis had continued to come without Andi, he no longer bothered to decorate. The decorating was likely for the kids' benefit rather than his own.

Bryce stepped from the woods and moved toward the house. Andi had forgotten to turn on the porch light for him, but a glow seeped around the edge of the drapes hanging at the front window. Knowing how many lights were on the tree, he wasn't surprised.

He knocked and immediately called, "It's me."

A few seconds later, the door swung open. Cooper pushed past Andi to give him a nudge and a tail wag. After Bryce greeted his dog, Andi stepped back to allow him entry. True to her word, she was dressed in the cat pajamas.

"Sorry. I'm going for comfort." She grinned. "Comfort and maybe a little bit of rebellion."

He lifted a brow. "How's that?"

"You know my mom. She was all about appearances. From the time I was old enough to realize I was a girl, she made sure my hair was styled and I was dressed to meet the president. Of the country club, at least, if not the United States." She closed and locked the door behind him. "By age fifteen, that included makeup. If she could see me now, I think she'd figure out a way to come back, just to give me one more of her infamous lectures."

Bryce shook his head. No wonder Andi had enjoyed escaping to Murphy.

"No need to apologize. You look cute." Actually, she looked better than cute. This casual, playful version of Andi was much more appealing than the uptight, professional one. This was the Andi he'd fallen in love with so many years ago. He cleared his throat, reminding himself they were just friends.

"The tree looks great." He moved close enough to study the ornaments and lifted a hand to touch one.

That was the year Dennis had made little boxes out of poster board and let Andi and him turn them into miniature Christmas presents. Bryce had wrapped them in her grandmother's leftover quilting fabric and passed each one to Andi to decorate with ribbon, berries, spray-painted pine needles and tiny bows. If his guy friends ever learned of the activities he'd done over here, they'd have grounds for blackmail.

She walked farther into the room and sank onto the couch. "There's nothing like sitting in front of a fire in the wintertime in a pair of flannel pj's."

He followed her gaze. Behind the fireplace screen, flames danced atop neatly stacked logs. She'd helped

Dennis build a fire so many times, he wasn't surprised she could do it on her own.

When he moved to stand in front of the fireplace, Cooper plopped down at his feet. Heat rose, warming his hands, still cold from the walk over. Three stockings hung across the mantel, the left one in memory of the man who had been a father to both of them.

His chest clenched. Dennis Wheaton's death was going to leave a hole in more than just Andi's life.

He crossed the room to where she sat. "Knowing you'd pulled all this out, I was afraid I'd get here to find you sad."

"Believe me, I had a brief period of feeling sorry for myself, even had a good cry. But I never wallow in self-pity for long."

Yes, Andi had developed an amazing inner strength. He'd sensed it almost from the moment she arrived.

He sank onto the couch next to her, letting his arm rest behind her back. He had to agree with her remark about sitting in front of a fire in the wintertime.

A warmth that had nothing to do with burning logs filled his chest. The scene brought a sense of contentment that he hadn't felt in a long time. The tree, branches heavy with fond memories. The woman he loved, even if only in friendship, sitting next to him. His dog—the dog they were now sharing—lying on the hearth, against a backdrop of dancing flames.

This exact scene had hung on his dining room wall for the past five years. The impact was like a boulder crashing into him, and he was left with an odd sense of having been caught in a time warp. Andi's long-ago sketch had materialized right in front of him. Cooper was even curled up on the hearth, standing in for old Sport.

He closed his eyes, once again seventeen, sitting next to the woman he was sure he'd spend the rest of his life with. He curled his hands into fists, trying to capture and hang on to that moment in time, when the future was bright with promise and he hadn't yet made the biggest mistake of his life.

"I really messed up."

She didn't ask what he meant. Her thoughts were probably following the same track his were. "Don't worry about it. We've all made our share of bad decisions. When you broke up with me, I sort of understood." She turned to look at him. "I knew exactly what I wanted. I was even ready to defy my mother by not choosing the son of one of her society friends."

"Yeah, your mom wouldn't have been thrilled." His throat tightened with that same sense of inferiority he'd felt as the kid from the wrong side of the tracks falling in love with the rich girl.

"But we would have had my dad's blessing." She gave him a sad smile. "Anyway, even though you were the only boyfriend I'd ever had, I knew what I wanted. But I understand that you didn't."

"You'd seen the world. I'd barely been outside North Carolina. Your lifestyle seemed so worldly. I thought the only way I'd know you were the one was if I experienced life, dated some other girls."

"I actually understood all that, even at eighteen." She shifted her gaze to stare into the fire. "What I didn't understand…"

He waited for her to finish her thought. When she didn't, he finished it for her. "…was how I could move on so quickly."

"Yeah."

But he hadn't moved on. It had only appeared that way. "As soon as I walked back home from your house, I started having second thoughts, wondering if I'd made the right decision. I kept thinking, what if I came to realize you *were* the one and you'd already found someone else."

He heaved a sigh and continued. "An hour or two later, Carla showed up."

She'd lived catty-corner across Ranger for years. They'd played together as children and sometimes hung out as teens. Other than her comments about how crazy he was to tie himself to a long-distance relationship when there were all kinds of girls in Murphy, she hadn't made any moves on him. Or he'd been too dense to see them.

"We were sitting on the porch swing, talking. I told her I'd broken up with you so we could date other people but was afraid I'd made a mistake. She was determined to show me I hadn't."

Andi crossed her arms in front of her, pulling them tightly over her torso. "You looked like you were enjoying the lesson."

"Of course I was." He wasn't going to lie to her. "I was an eighteen-year-old guy. But when I looked up and saw you standing there at the edge of the woods, eyes filled with pain, I knew I'd just sealed shut the door to any possible reconciliation in the future. And I wanted to rip out my own heart."

He'd shoved Carla off his lap and hurried after Andi. Before he could catch her, she'd locked herself in her house and refused to come out. Thirty minutes later, she and Dennis were pulling out of the driveway, heading to Atlanta.

"I never got a chance to talk to you after that. I just

want you to know what you meant to me and how sorry I am that I hurt you. Over the years, I've kicked myself more times than I can count."

Her hands fell to her lap, and she looked up at him, searching his eyes. Was she looking for sincerity? If he was projecting one-fourth of what he felt, she'd know without a doubt.

He reached up to touch her cheek. "I never had any more to do with her after that. I couldn't look at her without thinking of what I'd done to you."

When he let his finger trail along her jaw, she closed her eyes. They'd agreed to be just friends. That was all she'd wanted.

And it was all he'd wanted, too. After everything Pam had put him through, he didn't have the energy to fight his way past Andi's barriers.

But he didn't feel any of those barriers now. And he wanted nothing more than to kiss her.

When she opened her eyes, they were filled with uncertainty. But there was something else. A cautious hope.

He leaned closer, and her eyes drifted shut again. His lips brushed hers, the briefest touch before she turned away.

She crossed her arms again. "I'm sorry. I'm not ready for this. I don't know that I ever will be."

He sighed. Her walls had gone right back up. Thinking they'd ever have more than friendship had been nothing but a pipe dream. The scars ran too deep.

"That's all right. I'm totally fine with just being friends." He'd temporarily lost his head. It wouldn't happen again.

A log shifted, sending sparks spiraling upward into

the chimney. Cooper looked behind him, then settled back down.

"I made some eggnog." Andi pushed herself to her feet and headed toward the kitchen. On her way past the CD player, she hit Play.

A half minute later, the refrigerator door opened and closed and glasses clanked against a backdrop of "Winter Wonderland."

"I also made macaroons."

She returned carrying a tray that held a platter of cookies, their glasses of eggnog and two small plates. As she bent to lay it on the coffee table, "Winter Wonderland" died mid-phrase, and the lights clicked off, leaving only the glow of the fire.

Bryce reached for Andi, tension spiking through him. "Stay here."

He pulled his flashlight from his pocket and clicked it on. There were no storms in the area. He'd stepped from his car under a clear sky, an almost half-moon casting its soft glow over the landscape. No reason for the power to go out.

But seemingly unexplainable power outages happened occasionally. Sometimes someone hit a power pole on the four-lane, or a transformer burned up, or a limb came down across a line.

"What happened?" Andi's voice was paper-thin, with an underlying quiver.

"I'm going to look out the side and see if there's light in my direction."

Leaving her sitting in the living room, cookies and eggnog untouched, he darted down the hall to the master bedroom. When he swept aside the curtains, his uneasiness ratcheted up several notches. A soft glow shone through the trees—his own porch light. His power was on.

So what happened to Andi's?

Out front, glass shattered, followed by an almost simultaneous scream. A long string of fast, ferocious barks punctuated the wail of the alarm. He dropped the curtains into place and ran from the room, panic pounding at his heels.

At the end of the hall, Andi yanked a blanket from the back of the couch, her frame silhouetted against the flames still dancing in the fireplace. But a glow seemed to come from somewhere else, too.

He ran into the room. Cooper was nowhere to be seen. Flames engulfed the love seat that separated the living room from the dining area. Andi swung the blanket down hard, and the fire spread over the front of the small couch to lick at the living room rug.

He grabbed the blanket from her. "Start a pan filling with water, then call 911. The alarm system might not do it." Although the battery backup was supplying power to the alarm, he wasn't counting on the phone lines not being cut.

As water ran in the kitchen, he beat the sofa over and over. When the blanket caught fire, he dropped it and stomped on it, along with the rug, which also had flames working their way across it.

"No dial tone." Andi's words were laced with panic.

A fair share transferred to him. Someone hadn't just cut her power. He'd also broken off contact with the outside world.

She ran around him to snatch her cell phone from the coffee table. They'd knocked both glasses of eggnog over. The cream-colored liquid spread across the table and dripped to the floor.

Andi straightened. "One bar." After frantically punching the screen, she pressed it to her ear.

When Bryce had the last of the fire beat out, Andi lowered the phone. "Not enough service to get through."

"We need to go to my house."

"I'm not leaving my place unattended."

"And I'm not leaving you here alone. After we make that call, we'll come back and keep watch until they arrive."

He hollered for the dog, who slunk into the room from the direction of the kitchen. Before leading Andi out the door, he hooked on Cooper's leash and drew his weapon. Outside, faraway sirens wailed. As he crossed his yard and climbed his porch steps, they grew closer.

Bryce locked the three of them inside and pulled out his phone. Maybe the emergency vehicles were for them, maybe not. He wouldn't leave it to chance. He dialed 911 and soon had the confirmation he wanted. The alarm company had picked up an interruption. Not getting an answer on Andi's cell number, they'd dispatched the police.

Bryce pocketed his phone and stared at Andi, preparing himself for a battle. The cat pajamas made her look relaxed and playful. But he wasn't deceived. She was going to be as adamant as she'd be wearing a power suit. "You're not going to be able to stay at your place."

"I know. I've got to get the window fixed, clean up the damage from the fire."

"You're not going to be able to stay after that, either."

She flung up her hands. "Why keep the house if I

can't use it?" Her volume was several decibels louder than normal.

He raised his voice to match hers. "And what good is the house if you're dead?"

She drew in a breath, the action seeming to calm her. "If these creeps wanted me dead, they'd have already succeeded."

She sank onto his couch. "Somebody doesn't want me here, and he's trying to scare me off. Maybe it's Matt. Maybe it's Drysdale. Maybe it's someone else entirely." She crossed her arms. "Whoever it is, it's not going to work."

He heaved a sigh and sat next to her. "Andi, come on. This isn't the time for stubbornness."

She stood and started to pace. When she spoke, her voice was low and controlled.

"All my life, my mother has tried to dictate everything I've done, from what I wore to the jobs I held to who I married. I'm through." She pointed toward the property next door. "That's my home. It's been in my family for four generations. No one's going to take it from me, and no one's going to make me leave. Eventually, they'll see that and give up."

"Or eliminate the obstacle."

"No one is going to try to kill me over it."

"What about your parents?"

She stopped her pacing. A shadow crossed her features and worry settled in her eyes.

Then determination pushed it aside. "Monday, I'm meeting with Angie to discuss the terms for buying her business. I'm not going to back out. I'm here to stay."

Bryce shook his head, anger rolling in his gut. He was faced with an impossible situation.

A very determined woman.

A possible killer.

And neither of them willing to step away.

Andrea's gaze circled the dimly lit room, and she sought out a clock. It sat on the nightstand next to her bed, one of those older-style ones with hands. Almost 9:10 a.m.

Wait, that wasn't her clock. Where was she? And why was she still sleeping at 9:00 a.m.?

She pushed herself upright, and the events of the prior night slammed into her with the force of a tidal wave. Someone had tried to burn her house down. If Bryce hadn't been there, they might have succeeded.

She swung her feet over the side of the bed. The scent of smoke wafted upward. She needed to wash her pajamas. They reeked. But since it was the only pair she'd brought, she'd worn them, smoke and all.

Bryce had offered to loan her a T-shirt and some sweatpants, but she'd turned him down. Sleeping in his clothes felt too…intimate.

More memories rushed forward, and she stifled a groan. He'd tried to kiss her. And she'd almost let him. What had she been thinking?

She hadn't been. She'd let all the emotion that went with Christmas muddle her brain.

Throughout the afternoon, she'd pulled one memory after another from the dusty old boxes. No wonder she'd been a puddle of mush by the time he'd arrived.

Then he'd piled that apology on top of her already volatile emotions. It had been so heartfelt, it had just about done her in.

Until last night, she'd never given him the opportunity

to explain. She'd run inside the house and told her father that she wanted to leave. *Now.* It wasn't until they were on Spur 60, headed toward home, that she'd opened up and spilled the whole painful story. Her dad had listened, offering sympathy but no advice. Another way he'd been the polar opposite of her mother.

In the next weeks, Bryce had tried. But she'd ignored his calls and deleted his texts without reading them.

His apology last night had touched her. But it didn't change anything. They already had a meaningful friendship. As far as anything deeper, it wasn't just a twelve-year-old wrong that was keeping her from falling in love.

Phil had never apologized. No sorry-I-hurt-you-but-I-don't-love-you-anymore sentiment. He'd said she was overreacting, that a lot of successful men slept with other women.

Maybe so. But she wasn't willing to share. As long as she remained single, she didn't have to worry about it.

She gathered some clean clothes from the bag she'd brought over a few hours ago. A hot shower would be pure bliss. Hopefully Bryce wouldn't mind her tying up his hall bath for a while.

When she opened the bedroom door, the scent of coffee lured her toward the kitchen. The shower could wait. She padded barefoot down the hall.

Bryce smiled at her over the top of his computer screen. He sat at the table, nursing his own cup of coffee. "Good morning, Sleeping Beauty."

She wrinkled her nose. She was so *not* Sleeping Beauty. "What are you up to?"

"Checking out the headlines."

She opened a cabinet door, then closed it and moved to a second one.

"Left of the sink."

"Thanks." She took down a mug painted with a white-water rafting scene and filled it. After adding some half-and-half from the carton in the fridge, she joined him at the table. "Did I make the news?"

"Not this news. I'm sure there'll be a story about the fire in next week's *Cherokee Scout*." He closed the laptop. "What's on your agenda for today?"

"Laundry, for starters. It was time anyway, but I've got to wash these pajamas before I wear them again."

"You won't be allowed back in your house until the investigation is finished."

"Wonderful."

"They may let you get some more things out of the unaffected rooms. But you'll need to wash your clothes here."

She took a sip of coffee, the heat warming her from the inside out. After calling 911 last night, they'd gone back over to her house to wait. Bryce had immediately figured out what had happened to her power. The shed door was open, the padlock snapped with bolt cutters. Inside, the fuse for the house had been pulled. The instant he pushed it back in, the lights came on. The phone wasn't as easy. Someone had cut the wires in the box mounted on the side of the house.

With the lights on, they'd been able to check out the damage. Charred remains of something lay in front of the love seat. Based on how quickly the fire had spread, Bryce suspected someone had soaked an object with gasoline and thrown it through the broken window.

The love seat itself was burnt beyond repair. So was the rug. She'd strip and refinish the hardwood floor. It needed to be done anyway. But there'd probably forever be a large area darker than the rest of the floor, a permanent reminder of how blessed she was not to have lost her home.

As far as who had set the fire, the list of suspects was short—Matt Langman and Melvin Drysdale. Would Matt go to that extent to try to scare her off? If he burned the house down, he could come onto her property anytime he wanted. There'd be no one there to stop him.

But that scenario seemed off. Leaving threatening notes, putting dead squirrels in mailboxes—that was Matt's style. Trying to burn down houses, especially with people in them, didn't fit. According to her dad, all Matt's crimes had been petty.

That left Drysdale as the more likely suspect. She drew her brows together.

Bryce studied her. "You look like the wheels are turning."

"Yeah. The last time Drysdale came by to try to push me into selling, he told me to hang on to his card because I'm going to find that this place isn't worth it. I thought he was talking about all the work. Now I think it was a warning."

"The investigators will be checking him out."

She nodded. She'd thrown his card away but had retrieved his number from the call log on her phone.

She finished her coffee, then washed her cup and put it back in the cabinet. If she was going to crash at Bryce's for a few days, she could at least be a neat houseguest. She snagged the clothes she'd laid on her dresser earlier and crossed the hall to the bathroom.

Thirty minutes later, she emerged, wet hair wrapped in a towel and all traces of smoke removed. When she reached the kitchen, Bryce was standing at the stove, stirring scrambled eggs. The toaster had been pulled away from the wall, and waves of heat rose from the two slots. A knife lay propped up on the edge of a butter dish. A plate already held two finished slices.

He looked over at her. "Feel better now?"

"You have no idea."

The toast popped up. "If you want to butter those last two, we're almost ready to eat."

She helped him get everything to the table, then sat in the chair adjacent to his. "Watching you with your laptop earlier got me thinking. I need to get mine and connect it to your Wi-Fi, or I need to borrow yours."

"I'm finished. Help yourself." He pushed it in her direction. "What do you want to look up?"

"Melvin Drysdale."

"My buddy already did."

"He was focusing on investigations, criminal history, stuff like that."

She slid her plate over and pulled the computer next to it. She could work and eat at the same time. She'd done it for years.

"So, what are *you* going to focus on?"

"Everything else."

She brought up the internet and typed Drysdale's name into a search engine. The first two results were obituaries. "Since he likely hasn't faked his death, we'll assume these aren't him."

Bryce slid his chair up next to her and pointed at the screen. "Melvin Drysdale, president and CEO of Choice Property Development."

"That matches what was on the card he gave me."

She spooned a couple of forkfuls of eggs into her mouth. Bryce was already a third of the way through his.

She scrolled a little farther. "Priscilla Drysdale, Wife of Real Estate Mogul Melvin Drysdale, Disappears."

She clicked the link and scanned the article. The information was the same as what Bryce's friend had relayed, but didn't include the fact Drysdale was a suspect.

There were links to several more articles about projects he'd been involved in, but nothing that jumped out as being important.

She opened a new window and filled in the search bar.

"North Carolina Division of Corporations database?"

"Just seeing if he has his hands in anything other than Choice Property Development." She would check Georgia, too. But since he was dead set on acquiring her North Carolina property, she figured she'd start there first.

She clicked the link, and the search screen for the Secretary of State appeared. She searched by company officials, then tried again by registered agents. Both produced no results.

"Now Georgia." She took another bite of eggs. They were rapidly moving toward the cool side. As often as she worked while eating, she was used to cold food, too.

When she'd brought up Georgia's search window, she typed "Melvin Drysdale" into the "Officer Name" field. The results showed six businesses.

Bryce leaned closer. "If those are all the same Melvin Drysdale, he's a pretty busy guy."

"Or *has been* a busy guy." She pointed to the last column. "Half of them show a status of dissolved. Only three are currently active."

One was Choice Property Development, which was no surprise. Drysdale was listed as the CEO. The other officers' names didn't ring a bell.

"Let's check out these businesses." She clicked the

back arrow. "Terra Minerals Limited." Her pulse kicked up speed as she clicked the link. "Sounds like a mining company. Drysdale is the chief financial officer."

"What kind of company is it?" Bryce's tone held some of her own excitement.

"That's not given here. Just says 'Domestic Profit Corporation.' I'm sure they have a website."

Fifteen seconds later, she'd navigated to the page. "Bingo. They're a mining operation. No wonder Drysdale is so determined to get his hands on my property."

Had Matt found gold and blabbed it to the wrong people? Knowing him, he'd embellished the story. A lot.

She looked at Bryce, mind spinning. "Drysdale may have tried to buy the property from my dad. Then when my dad refused, Drysdale had both of my parents killed, figuring with my life in Atlanta, I'd be happy to unload the property."

"You might be getting ahead of yourself. Are you sure Terra Minerals actually mines gold?"

She clicked on "About Us" and scanned the company information. Disappointment doused the excitement she'd felt moments earlier. "They mine kaolin."

"What's kaolin?"

"China clay. It's used in making china and other tableware, but its biggest use is in the paper industry."

He looked at her with raised brows. "How do you know this stuff?"

"I did a research paper on mining my freshman year of high school. Earth science."

"And you remember."

She shrugged. "They mine a lot of it in Georgia." She pulled her lower lip between her teeth. "But mining kaolin is nothing like mining gold. It's not likely that one company would do both."

"Unless Drysdale is involved in two different companies."

She clicked the back arrow. "Nope. The other one is Executive Group Financial Services, definitely not a gold mine." She shook her head. "Property development, mining and financial services. Drysdale's got his hands in a little bit of everything."

She followed the link to check out the last company. "He's the vice president on this one." She shifted her gaze to the name above Drysdale's and gasped. "John Lassiter. One of my dad's business partners."

"Could be a different John Lassiter."

"And a different Mark Barrand as CFO?"

Bryce nodded. "Okay, that's too much coincidence."

When she read the last name, a dark heaviness descended on her, wrapping her in dread. "My dad is listed as the secretary. Why wouldn't he have told me he was a principal in another endeavor?" She looked at Bryce, silently pleading for an explanation that didn't put a stain on her father's integrity. He didn't offer any.

She shifted her gaze back to the computer screen. "When Drysdale first showed up, he said he saw the obituary, and that's how he knew the property might be for sale. But he and my dad were in business together, along with my dad's two partners. Why didn't he mention that?"

The same reason her father hadn't. Nausea churned in her stomach, and she put a hand over her mouth. The breakfast she'd managed to consume between clicks was threatening to make a reappearance.

"When was the company formed?"

She lowered her hand. "Two years ago."

"About a year before the big money started coming in." Bryce's voice sounded tight, pinched. He obviously didn't want to believe it any more than she did.

So everything wasn't about gold.

Or maybe it was. If her father mentioned the presence of gold on his property to one of his business partners and that person mentioned it to Drysdale, Drysdale might have decided to have it checked out. Maybe he learned the Wheatons were sitting on a small fortune, one he was determined to have for himself.

As improbable as her theory sounded, that was the explanation she'd cling to. Because the alternative was unthinkable. Her sweet, honest father would never have been involved in anything shady.

There had to be a legitimate reason for the financial success he'd seen within months of forming the new company.

And a logical reason why he'd chosen to keep those details from her.

TEN

The dryer buzzed, and Andrea strode into the laundry room off the side of the kitchen. It felt good to be home. She'd been there the past three days.

Last Friday she'd learned that investigators had finished collecting evidence, and she was free to return to the house. It helped that the damage had been confined to such a small area.

The fire was still under investigation. Bryce knew the investigators. Actually, he seemed to know everybody. Although he'd gotten them to promise to notify her of anything they found, she wasn't expecting any earth-shattering news. What happened was pretty clear-cut. Someone had broken a window and thrown a flaming object inside. What she really wanted to know was who. No lab tests were likely to reveal that.

She opened the dryer door and removed her bedspread. She'd finished her clothes on Saturday, her smoky pajamas two days before that. Those, Bryce had thrown in with his own smoky clothes. Today she was tackling the bedding. Since she and Bryce had beat out the fire before smoke could fill the house, it probably wasn't necessary. But it made her feel better.

Things were almost back to normal. The phone company had replaced severed wires, and Bryce had padlocked the box. She'd also called the same handyman who'd replaced the window after the first break-in. She'd be using him on some future projects, too. Especially ones that involved ladders.

She headed down the hall with the still warm bedspread. She'd received another call on Friday, too—regarding her parents' accident. The investigation had been inconclusive. The underside of the car had simply been too mangled, brake lines ripped loose along with everything else. If there'd been any brake fluid left on the ground where they'd parked at the lodge, several hard rains had destroyed the evidence before any questions had been raised.

She'd just finished putting the bedspread on her bed when a knock sounded on the front door. That would be Bryce, with Cooper.

When she opened the door, the dog almost knocked her down bounding inside. He made two circles around the living room, then stood, looking up at her, body quivering with excitement.

She dropped to one knee and cupped his face. "What's this all about? You just saw me this morning."

"I think he got spoiled having both of us for a couple of days." Bryce's smile died. "You already know how I feel about you coming back home."

Yeah, she did. He'd made it clear. She'd also made her thoughts on the matter clear. "If I'm going to let these creeps run me off, I might as well sell the property to Drysdale."

Before he could offer any further argument, her cell phone rang, and she swiped it from the coffee table. Tension crept across her shoulders. She didn't recognize the number.

After she gave a tentative "Hello," the caller identified himself as Gilbert Ormand, the fire investigator. They weren't finished, but he was calling to give her what they had so far.

She glanced at Bryce. It helped to know people who knew people.

As Ormand talked, she paced. Bryce stood leaning against the doorjamb, watching her, arms crossed.

"We didn't get any viable prints from around the window. And with the hardness of the ground and the fact that it's covered in leaves this time of year, there weren't any footprints left behind."

Andrea sighed. Two pieces of evidence that could point to who was trying to scare her off.

Mr. Ormand continued. "There was an almost empty gas can against the side of the house, a short distance from where the fire was started. Several prints were lifted from that and came back belonging to Matthew Langman."

Andrea stopped pacing, her jaw lax. "He's my neighbor. He's threatened me several times."

"Yeah, that's what Bryce said. Police talked to Matthew and his father. The younger Langman claimed his gas can had gone missing the day before. Langman Senior gave his son an alibi, said he'd sat in the living room all evening, playing with the Xbox."

So Matt had an alibi. His father. Which, in Andrea's opinion, wasn't an alibi at all. Ormand went on to say that Drysdale had an alibi, too. His was more convincing. But that might only mean he had someone else doing his dirty work.

"The arsonist tied a bunch of rags around a rock, so it would throw well, then soaked everything in gasoline and lit it."

Andrea nodded. That was no surprise. Seeing the charred blob lying there, she'd assumed as much.

When she ended the call, Bryce looked at her with raised brows. "Well?"

"They found a gas can. Guess whose prints were all over it."

"Matt's."

"Of course, Matt claims someone stole it, and his old man has given him an alibi."

"Why am I not surprised?"

She took a seat on the couch. "If Matt *is* the one behind all this, he's not working alone. There are at least two others."

Bryce sat next to her. "The two who broke into your house."

"Right. And Drysdale. I have no idea what his involvement is, but as badly as he wants my property, I'm sure he's connected somehow."

"We already know he was involved with your father."

"That, too." She drew in a deep breath. "Ormand said he has an alibi during the time of the fire. He'd taken a girlfriend out to dinner in Atlanta and dropped her off at home at nine thirty, which doesn't give him enough time to have made the trip to Murphy. She corroborated his story. So did the restaurant."

"He could still have someone working for him, like the two guys who broke into your house."

"My thoughts exactly." She crossed her arms. "Matt probably knows a lot more than he's letting on. Eventually he's going to mess up."

"Like leaving the gas sitting where he used it?"

"Yeah. That's a major careless mistake. He probably soaked everything, then laid the can down. By the time he broke the window, set the ball of rags on fire and tossed it into my house, his focus was on getting out of there, and he forgot to pick up the gas can." She gave Bryce a wry smile. "I think all the drugs he's taken have killed a few too many brain cells."

She pushed herself to her feet. "I'd better get ready for my appointment with Angie. I'd hate to go looking like this."

"There's nothing wrong with the way you look."

The warmth in his tone sent goose bumps cascading over her. When she met his gaze, the same heat was reflected in his eyes. She crossed the room, ignoring the effect his obvious appreciation had on her.

"I'm in sweats and no makeup. I've spent the morning cleaning house and doing laundry." But that made no difference to him. He'd always thought she looked good and had never hesitated to say so. It touched a chord with her now even more than it had then.

She tamped down the longing and grinned at him over one shoulder. "Remind me not to rely on you for fashion advice."

He laughed. "I'm a guy. That's usually not one of our strong points."

He headed toward the door and she followed, ready to lock it behind him.

"By the time you come home tonight, you'll be living next door to the proud new owner of Designs by Angie. Or maybe I should say Designs by Andi. At least the negotiations will be underway."

His face lit with a smile of his own. "I'm proud of you."

"Why?" Being director of marketing for a Fortune 500 company, dozens of people under her, was a lot more impressive than taking over a tiny one-woman operation in Murphy, North Carolina.

"You're stepping out of your comfort zone, embarking on a new life. It takes a lot of guts to do that."

Her heart swelled with the approval in his eyes. He seemed to instinctively know what a woman needed. What *she* needed. Too bad he wasn't willing to expend the energy required to develop a relationship. And too bad she wasn't willing to let down her guard enough to try again.

After he left, she strode toward her room to get ready. Fortunately, her ankle was pretty well healed. A week earlier, and she'd have been limping into the store with a walking stick.

When she returned to the living room, Cooper had jumped up on the couch and was stretched out across two-thirds of its length.

She planted her hands on her hips. "Does your daddy let you up on the furniture? I don't think so." She pointed at the floor. "Down."

The dog obeyed but looked at her with sad eyes. Bryce had assured her he wouldn't destroy the house while she was gone. Since Bryce would be leaving for work before she returned, he'd had to bring the dog over before she left.

"All right. I'll go get your bed." Bryce had bought a second one to keep at his house so the original could stay at hers. After plopping it down in front of the hearth and checking the water bowl, she headed out the door.

Tomorrow she was going car shopping. Maybe she'd even go this afternoon. There was a GM dealership in Murphy.

She'd pretty much decided to get another Escalade, maybe in a different color. Her old one was gray, a hue Cadillac had named Bronze Dune Metallic. Now she wanted something bolder, something that reflected her new sense of adventure. Red. Metallic red, if that was an option.

She slid into the rental car, tossing her purse into the passenger seat. After pulling onto Ranger, she gave it a little gas, allowing the car to gradually gain speed as she wound downward toward the four-lane.

Halfway there, she tapped the brake going into a curve. Something didn't feel right. The pedal was squishy. A second later, it hit the floor.

Her heart leaped into her throat. She pumped the brake several times. Now there was no resistance at all. When she yanked on the emergency brake, nothing happened.

Panic pounded through her as she continued to gain speed, tombstones on both sides of her a blur. The road made a sharp curve left, the steep slope to the right deep enough to roll the car if she didn't make it.

She slid around the final curve, tires squealing. As she shot onto the four-lane, she swiveled her head to the left. The huge grill of a semitruck bore down on her. The horn blared, blending with her own scream. She barely cleared the truck's path as it skidded past behind her.

She flew across the break in the median and became temporarily airborne as she cleared the slightly raised eastbound lanes. Any speed she'd lost crossing the four-lane, she quickly regained on Little Ranger Road's downhill slope. Another sharp curve was just ahead of her, to the right this time.

She was going too fast to make it. Her tires lost traction and she skidded across the oncoming lane.

A chain-link fence stood ahead of her, trees looming just behind it. A half second later, her whole world exploded in white.

Then everything went black.

Bryce walked up his driveway, flipping through the envelopes he'd just retrieved from the mailbox. Mostly junk. He'd toss those into the trash, unopened, as soon as he got inside. The rest...

The wail of a distant siren pulled his thoughts from the mail. Uneasiness trickled through him. Sirens in Murphy weren't a common occurrence, especially this far from town.

He rolled his shoulders in a slow circle, trying to dispel some of the tension. Andi would have left fifteen or twenty minutes ago. She was probably in town already, pulling up to the store.

The wail grew louder. Another one joined the first, rising and falling in a different pattern. Bryce knit his brows. There was more than one emergency vehicle.

He pulled his phone from his pocket. He'd check to make sure Andi was all right. Then he'd be able to get on with his afternoon, which in another hour would involve heading to work.

After bringing her up on his contact list, he touched the screen and put the phone to his ear. It rang once. Twice.

The sirens reached their loudest, faded slightly, then

fell silent. His stomach tightened. That was close, like just past where Ranger met the four-lane.

Andi's phone rang a third time. Then a fourth. When her message came on, he disconnected the call and closed the distance to his Sorento at a jog. The sirens likely had nothing to do with Andi. Maybe she was still driving and would call him back when she stopped. Or maybe she'd arrived at the store early and was already in her meeting.

But it wouldn't be that difficult to put his mind at ease.

After cranking the SUV, he backed to the right and jammed the vehicle into Drive, kicking up gravel as he shot toward the road.

When he reached the four-lane, he almost crumpled in relief. Lights flashed on the opposite side, a hundred feet or so ahead on Little Ranger Road. Andi would have pulled into the median and made a left to head toward town. She'd have had no reason to continue straight.

He waited for a vehicle to pass, then crossed the highway. The Ranger Community Center was just ahead, a good place to turn around. He pressed the brake, ready to make his left into the center, but then changed his mind. The emergency vehicles weren't far beyond it. The victims could be people he knew.

As he approached, he slowed to a crawl. A Cherokee County Sheriff unit was stopped along one side of the road, an ambulance on the other. He drove slowly between.

When he looked left, his heart stuttered. Just past the ambulance, the chain-link fence that ran along that side of the road was mangled, a section of it missing. Down the slope beyond, the rear end of a car was barely visible. Dark blue, like Andi's.

He whipped the Sorento off the road in front of the sheriff vehicle. *God, please don't let it be Andi.*

No, it couldn't be Andi. She knew which way town was.

He jumped from the car and ran across the road. Definitely a Honda Accord. It had sailed through the fence, sideswiped several trees, then come to an abrupt stop against two others. He skidded down the gentle slope to where emergency personnel were working to extract the driver. He wouldn't disturb them or get in their way. He just needed to know whether it was Andi inside.

When he circled around to the front of the car and looked through the windshield, he had to grab the hood to stay on his feet.

It *was* Andi. Her head was tipped to the side, her eyes closed. Blood trailed from a gash on the side of her face, soaking into her blouse.

A paramedic standing at the open driver's door carefully lifted her head and held it steady while another one fastened a brace around her neck. Bryce stood with his heart in his throat, watching them work to stabilize her.

Another figure moved down the slope toward him. Sam Williamson, dressed in Cherokee County garb. He'd started with the department about a year ago, working patrol.

Sam tilted his head toward the car. "You know her?"

"She's…my neighbor." His neighbor, and so much more.

"Any idea what happened? To have struck this hard, this close to the four-lane, she had to have come off Ranger Road flying."

He shook his head. "She was headed to town. She should have turned at the highway."

Instead, she'd gone straight through without stopping. *Because she didn't have any brakes.*

Realization slammed into him. Someone cut her brake lines. Whoever was after her didn't just want her gone from Murphy.

He wanted her dead. The same as her parents.

Her mom had missed a curve and driven off the side of a mountain. Andi told him the investigation was inconclusive. But he didn't need investigative results to know what had happened. Mrs. Wheaton had missed a curve because someone had tampered with the Mercedes's brakes.

He grasped Sam's forearm. "Make sure they check her brakes. And she needs around-the-clock protection at the hospital."

Sam lifted his brows. "That's some pretty serious stuff."

"Believe me, some serious things have been happening. We can't let her out of our sight."

He wasn't going to let her out of his. He had three weeks of vacation banked. If he had to use every bit of it protecting Andi, he'd do it.

This was just what he'd feared. Dennis wouldn't sell the Murphy property, so someone had removed him as an obstacle. That same person was now going after Andi. With no one else to inherit, the estate would likely be liquidated and the property would go to the highest bidder.

Bryce placed the call to the department. He'd do an official vacation request later, but this would cover him for today. Finally, the paramedics had Andi removed from the car and stretched out on a spine board, ready to load her into the ambulance. She was still unconscious.

"You're taking her to Murphy Medical?" He knew

both paramedics. He'd gone all the way through school with one and worked some accidents with the other.

"Yeah, for now. We've got her stabilized. If necessary, she'll be transferred to a trauma unit."

After shooting off a quick text to both Tanner and Colton, he headed for the hospital. When he arrived, the only information he was able to get was that the doctor was sending her to X-ray.

He took a seat in the waiting room and checked his phone. Tanner and Colton had both texted him back. Tanner still had another couple of hours to finish his shift but was going to try to cut out early. Colton was on his way. A district attorney, he apparently wasn't in court this afternoon.

Within minutes, the automatic glass door opened, and Colton walked into the emergency waiting room. "What happened?"

"She was going to town. Missed the curve on Little Ranger."

Colton's brows knitted as he took a seat. "Little Ranger? What was she doing over there?"

"My thoughts exactly. I haven't talked to her, but I think I know what happened. She got to the bottom of Ranger and had no brakes. In light of everything that's happened, I believe someone tampered with them."

Colton frowned. "She shouldn't be staying there alone."

Bryce released a frustrated breath. "Try telling her that. She's developed a stubborn streak a mile wide."

His leg began to bounce, heel tapping against the floor. "She has an alarm system. I've secured the house as best as I can. I've even got Cooper sleeping with her to alert her if anyone tries to come in. But I'm still about to go out of my mind worrying about her."

Colton's eyes widened and understanding filtered in. "That's her, isn't it?"

"What do you mean?"

"The one you told us about. You've never gotten over her."

Bryce heaved a sigh. There was no use trying to evade the question.

"Yeah, that's her." And now that she was lying injured on a gurney somewhere in the hospital, he realized how much she still meant to him.

By the time the doctor came out to talk with him, Bryce's nerves were coiled so tightly he almost sprang from the chair.

"She's awake, but disoriented, which is understandable. We've run X-rays and a CT scan. We don't have the results yet, but you can go back and see her now."

He followed the doctor, leaving Colton sitting in the waiting room. When the doctor slid the curtain back on its track, Bryce stepped around him into the small area.

His knees went weak as shock collided with relief. A figure was lying on the small bed, sheet tucked around her, head held immobile by a cervical collar. Small cuts and abrasions marked her face and arms, and a decent-sized bruise seemed to be forming on one cheek. The spine board they'd used at the scene was still beneath her.

His heart twisted. She looked so small and frail, encased in plastic and linen. He drew closer.

She was awake, staring at the ceiling. The collar didn't offer her any other option. Her eyes shifted to meet his and the edges of her mouth lifted in the start of a smile. It was small, barely noticeable. But it melted his heart.

He loved this woman. He could no longer deny it. He'd told himself that he'd be content with nothing more than friendship.

But somewhere between that conversation in her living room and today's accident, everything had changed.

No matter how much he'd tried to fight it, he'd fallen in love with her all over again.

Or maybe he hadn't. Through the long years apart, as she'd married and had her life and he'd gotten on with his, maybe he'd never stopped loving her.

Maybe deep down, in some sectioned-off corner of his heart, too painful to explore, he'd loved her all along.

ELEVEN

Bryce pulled away from Murphy Medical Center, Andi next to him.

She crossed her arms and leaned back in the seat. "I can't believe they kept me for three days."

"The doctor was concerned about your memory loss." When she'd first woken up, the events surrounding the accident were a complete blank. She remembered cautioning Cooper to be good and walking out the door. The next thing she was aware of was waking up in the ambulance on the way to the hospital.

"By the next morning, I was completely back to normal. Mentally, anyway. I feel like I've been run over by a truck."

"No trucks. But you did do battle with several trees."

She shifted position and winced. "I think they won." She paused. "I need to go back to the house."

"Andi, we talked about this." She'd agreed to stay with her aunt and uncle in Asheville, two hours away. He'd packed her clothing into her two suitcases and currently had them in his back seat, along with her laptop. Meanwhile, Cherokee County deputies would watch her place, hoping to catch whoever was behind the attacks.

Yesterday, they'd gotten some preliminary results of the investigation. The cable to the emergency brake had been cut. The other lines hadn't, as he'd initially suspected. Instead, someone had loosened both bleeder screws on the driver's side. After she'd slowed two or three times, there wouldn't have been enough brake fluid left to stop the car.

Investigators hadn't found the tool used to cut the emergency brake cable, but a bleeder wrench lay a short distance from the gravel drive, partially concealed by dried leaves. They'd lifted prints but didn't have the results back yet.

Andi held up a hand. "Don't worry. I haven't changed my plans. I just need to get some stuff."

"It's not safe."

"When I come back, the house may not even still be standing. There are pictures and things there that I can't replace, memories of my father."

He heaved a sigh. "Fifteen minutes max. And we'll wait for backup." He pulled over to make the call, then headed toward Ranger.

When he turned off the four-lane, instead of traveling up the road, he pulled into Ranger United Methodist Church's parking lot. On a Thursday afternoon, it was empty. After circling the lot, he stopped to wait at the entrance. The church sat high on the hill to his left, its cemetery sprawling beside and in front of him.

His cell phone rang, and he pulled it from his pocket. The call was from the detective in charge of her case.

Bryce's pulse kicked up. "Any new developments?"

"We got an ID on the prints we lifted from the wrench. Matt Langman."

"Have you talked to him?"

"Yeah. Same as before. He checked his tools and said his wrench is missing."

"Has he been arrested?"

"We kept him for questioning, then released him. Since he leaves everything outside, easily accessible to anyone, the evidence wasn't strong enough to hold him."

Bryce nodded. Either Matt's threats were getting much more serious, or someone was setting him up. He was inclined to believe the latter. The gas can and wrench left behind were too convenient.

He disconnected the call and filled Andi in on the details. He'd just finished when a cruiser turned onto Ranger. He followed it to the Wheaton house. While one deputy kept watch outside, the other waited in the living room.

After boxing up some photo albums and mementos Andi and Dennis had collected, they pulled ornaments from the tree, leaving it essentially bare. They all had sentimental value, since they were handmade. Finally, everything Andi wanted to keep was boxed up. They loaded the items into his truck and thanked the deputies.

In two hours, they'd be in Asheville. Though Andi had initially wanted to go back to her condo in Atlanta, he'd talked her out of it. That would be the first place her attackers would check.

He followed the cruiser up the drive. At the end of Ranger, it pulled into the median, ready to complete a left turn.

Bryce waited for two vehicles to pass. By the time he was ready to pull out, the cruiser was moving down the highway, headed toward town.

He lifted his foot from the brake. Before he could step on the gas, Andi gasped.

He swiveled his head to look at her. "What?"

"I've figured it out. My dad's note. Turn around."

After a glance in his rearview mirror, he backed into a drive on their right. But he wasn't leaving the safety of the vehicle until he knew what she had in mind.

Excitement radiated from her. "I've felt all along that Dad left the note for a reason. It was a message to me. He wanted to tell me something that wouldn't be obvious to anyone else."

Yeah, it wasn't obvious to him, either. He drew to a stop in her driveway. "Go ahead."

"My dad talked about burying secrets deep. I've wondered all along if he meant it figuratively or literally. Now I know. He physically buried something."

Bryce frowned. "If it was buried deep, like the note said, I don't know of anywhere on your ten acres that that could have been accomplished easily. I think I proved that burying the squirrel."

Andi turned in the seat to face him more fully. "I don't think he had to dig the hole. I think it was already dug."

"What do you mean?" His jaw went lax. "The well."

What was it Andi had told him? Dennis had said that instead of collecting wishes, the well collected burdens.

She reached for the door handle, but he held up a hand. "Wait."

Her shoulders dropped. "No one's here. Your friend already checked everything out."

She was right. Gary had circled the house the entire time they'd been inside and had seen no one.

"We'll be back on the road in no time." Her eyes were pleading. "I just have to know before we head to Asheville. You can even stand guard with your gun."

She climbed from the truck, and he got out the other side. "Wait."

But she was already headed around the side of the house at a jog. He followed her into the woods, weapon drawn and eyes peeled for any signs of movement.

It was dusk. They had maybe another twenty minutes of daylight left. If Andi was right, they'd have what they wanted in five.

When they reached the well, Andi pulled the bucket up, hand over hand on the rope. As she worked, he continued to cast glances around them.

Finally, she grasped the bucket's handle and looked inside. Her face fell. "It's empty. I thought for sure this was it, that we'd find the answer here."

She set the bucket on the edge of the well. It leaned at an angle, as if the bottom wasn't flat. When she turned it over, something was affixed there with pieces of duct tape, crisscrossed over one another.

Bryce's pulse kicked into overdrive. Dennis had probably died for whatever was taped to the bottom of that bucket. And whoever killed Dennis wouldn't hesitate to take out him and Andi, as well.

He scanned the woods again and froze. Had he just seen movement near the back of the property?

He tightened his grip on the pistol. "We need to go. Now."

"Not without this." Andi pried one end loose and, with a jerk, peeled the whole thing back. The rip of glue letting go seemed to echo in the silence.

Then there was another sound, much closer than where he'd seen movement earlier.

This one turned his blood to ice.

It was the telltale click of a hammer being pulled back on a revolver.

Another click followed and a third.

Icy fingers danced down Andrea's spine. She'd never been around guns. But she'd watched enough detective shows to know what she'd just heard. Even if she hadn't, Bryce's expression would have given it away. Every bit of color had drained from his face.

"There's three of us and two of you." The words came from beyond them, deeper in the woods. The voice belonged to Drysdale.

She stood frozen, too afraid to move. Bryce had wanted to wait for backup. She'd been in too much of a hurry.

Dear God, what have I done?

Drysdale spoke again. "Drop the gun and kick it away from you."

After several moments' hesitation, Bryce did as he'd been told.

"Now hands in the air."

Andrea raised her arms, still holding the package, and watched Drysdale approach. Two men flanked him. One was huge. They all held pistols. Though only Drysdale had spoken, she was pretty sure the others were the two who'd ransacked her place.

"Now head toward the house. If either of you try anything, we'll shoot you both."

"Here, take it." Andrea shook what was in her hand—a small padded envelope, folded in half, duct tape stuck to one side. "You can have the gold. Take anything you're able to pull out of the mine. I don't want it."

Drysdale snatched the package from her hand with a condescending snort. "Do you really think this is all over a few gold nuggets?"

Dread trickled over her. When she'd learned about the gold, she'd clung to that theory with every bit of determination she had. It hadn't been the most practical explanation. But it had been better than considering the alternative, that her father had gotten involved in something illegal and finally decided to clear his conscience.

"Now move. We're going in the front door."

Drysdale's command sliced across her thoughts. She obeyed, Bryce walking next to her.

"I need my keys. They're in Bryce's truck, in my purse." So was her phone. Maybe she'd have an opportunity to slip it into her pocket and eventually get off a quick 911 call.

Drysdale marched them around the side of the house and into the driveway. She'd left her purse on the front floorboard. After opening the passenger door, she leaned in and unzipped it, but before she could slip her hand inside, Drysdale's voice stopped her.

"Wait. Bring it out here where we can see you."

Her heart fell. So much for trying to retrieve her phone. She straightened and pulled her keys from the front pouch.

"Now toss your purse back into the vehicle."

She did as Drysdale commanded, then let the armed men direct her toward her front door. Maybe she could enter the alarm code incorrectly and pass it off as nervousness.

As soon as she opened the front door, the alarm sounded its entry tone, waiting for the code. Her hand shook as she lifted it to the panel.

Drysdale spoke close to her ear. "Think about what you're doing, because if the alarm goes off, we'll shoot you both right here."

She punched in the four numbers and the alarm fell silent. When she cast a glance at Bryce, his eyes were alert and tension radiated from him. The two of them were outnumbered and unarmed. But if any opportunity for escape presented itself, Bryce would be all over it.

"Python, find something to bind the cop."

Drysdale's words sent panic spiraling through her. With Bryce tied up, their chances of escape would plummet.

The larger man looked around him. "What?"

"Rope, tape, anything."

There was no rope inside, but the desk drawer held duct tape. If the men were the same ones who'd ransacked her house, they'd know that.

After a moment's hesitation, the man called Python walked to the desk, then opened and closed drawers until he found the right one. Drysdale made a motion with his pistol.

"Tape his hands behind him."

After laying his weapon on the bookcase, he grabbed one of Bryce's wrists. When Bryce resisted, he gave that arm a twist. Bryce winced but didn't make a sound. At a well-muscled six foot two, Bryce wasn't a small guy. But Python was huge. He'd probably gotten the nickname because of the size of his arms.

Two seconds later, Andrea was trapped against the smaller man's chest, his arm around her throat and the cold barrel of the pistol pressed against her temple.

Words hissed against her ear. "If you don't wanna see your girlfriend's brains blown all ova this room, you betta do what you're told." It was the New Englander with the attitude.

Bryce put his hands behind his back and allowed the man to tape his wrists together. But the determination in his eyes was unmistakable.

The New Englander lowered the gun but didn't release her. She watched, helpless, while Python shoved Bryce backward onto the couch and taped his ankles.

What were they going to do, shoot them? No, if that was their plan, they'd have done it outside and left their bodies in the woods. They had something else in mind.

Bryce didn't deserve any of it. She should never have let him get involved. She looked at Drysdale. "What do you want? The property? I'll sell it to you. In fact, I'll give it to you. Just let Bryce go. He has nothing to do with this."

"I don't want the property."

"You've hounded me to sell it to you. Let Bryce go, and I'll sign it over to you, no strings attached."

"I don't need the property anymore. I'm guessing everything I want is in this little package."

"Then take it and leave." Bryce's tone was cold and commanding. "You're already under investigation for the murder of Dennis and Margaret Wheaton. You might get away with it. But if you follow through with whatever you have planned here, there'll be nowhere you can run that they won't find you."

Ignoring Bryce, Drysdale nodded toward Python. "Shut him up."

Python balled up one meaty fist and drew it back. Andrea released a shriek, which was cut abruptly short as the other man clamped his hand over her mouth.

"No, the tape, you idiot." Drysdale's tone was sharp. "I want him conscious."

As Python tore off a six-inch strip of duct tape and pressed it over Bryce's mouth, Drysdale removed a folding knife from his pocket and sliced open the envelope. Inside was a zippered plastic bag. He pulled out the contents, and Andrea held her breath. Whatever her father had hidden, he'd wrapped it in several paper towels. Drysdale unfolded them, dropping each to the floor, then held up a thumb drive. "Where is your computer?"

"In Bryce's truck." She cast a sideways glance at the man still holding her. "He and I can go get it."

Maybe she'd have another shot at getting her phone.

"You stay here." The command came from Drysdale. "Slater, go get it."

So that was the New Englander's name. It could be a nickname, like Python, but it wouldn't hurt to remember it.

Slater released her and moved toward the door. As he turned to throw the dead bolt, her gaze slid to his shoes. They were tennis shoes, worn and dirty. She'd seen them before. Had he been wearing them while he'd ransacked her room as she hid under the bed?

She couldn't remember. She'd been too terrified to notice details.

He disappeared out the front door, then came back a minute later with her laptop. Drysdale pushed aside a water glass she'd left sitting on the coffee table and opened her laptop. After taking a seat on the other end of the couch from Bryce, he booted up the computer and inserted the thumb drive.

She'd give almost anything to learn what was on that drive, but she couldn't see the screen from where she stood. Python and Slater were positioned on either side of her, their weapons tucked into the waistbands of their jeans. But judging from their alert stances, neither had let down his guard.

Her father had probably uncovered some things that could send Drysdale and his partners to prison and had saved the evidence, intending to show it to Bryce.

Was his hesitation in going straight to the Atlanta police because he was struggling over having to turn in his partners?

Or was the struggle over turning himself in?

For several minutes, Drysdale leaned forward, scanning whatever was there. Finally, he looked up, nodding. "Just what we suspected. Lassiter was right. When he found Dennis at the office late on a Saturday night, he knew he was up to something. He was acting too weird." He closed the cover, and his gaze met Andrea's. "The man has good instincts. He followed your dad, figured out he was headed up here."

Andrea pursed her lips. So why didn't Lassiter just follow her dad all the way to Murphy and get what he wanted? Because men like Drysdale and Lassiter never did their own dirty work. They always had others do it for them.

Drysdale continued. "Lassiter said we needed to have his office and cell phones bugged. It paid off."

The pieces of the puzzle started to click into place. One of her dad's partners had listened in on his conversation with Bryce. Then they'd had to come up with a way to silence him before that meeting could take place.

Drysdale nodded to Python. "Restrain her, too."

As the man jerked her hands behind her back, Drysdale shook his head. "I would never have expected that out of Dennis. What kind of man double-crosses his partners?"

Andrea stared down at Drysdale, eyes narrowed. "You should have known better than to bring in someone like my dad. As smart as he was, he was bound to figure out what you were up to, and he was too honest and upright to keep quiet."

Drysdale's face reddened, and he sprang to his feet. She'd obviously hit a nerve.

"If you think dear daddy was so honest and upright, you need to be enlightened." He circled the coffee table, grabbed her by the hair and forced her to her knees.

Bryce slid forward on the couch and struggled to his feet. Python shoved him back down, then stepped up beside Drysdale.

"Come on, boss, we need to do what we came for and get out of here."

Do what we came for?

"No. I want her to know what kind of man her father really was." He turned the laptop around and opened the cover. A long list of files filled the screen, many titled "Geological Report," each followed by an address.

Had someone done a geological report on her family's property and found the probability of a rich gold vein? But Drysdale had said it wasn't about the gold.

Bending at the waist, he clicked on a file titled "Investors." A spreadsheet appeared, line after line of names, dates and amounts.

She looked at the entries more closely. With each name, there were dates with funds taken in, and much larger amounts paid out three months later. Drysdale scrolled down, where increasingly more investors were listed.

It didn't take Andrea long to assign meaning to what she was looking at. Drysdale and his partners were involved in a Ponzi scheme. Maybe her father had been, too. The realization was like a kick to the gut.

If he'd been involved, there was one consolation. He'd gathered the evidence, brought it here and contacted Bryce. Law enforcement. Maybe he *had* allowed himself to get caught up in the scheme. But he'd made the decision to turn everything over to the authorities.

Drysdale closed the folder with a smirk. "So your father wasn't so pious after all."

Maybe he wasn't. But he'd done the right thing in the end.

Drysdale nodded at Python. "Finish restraining her."

Python shoved her sideways, and her head hit the floor with a thud. While large hands wrapped tape around her ankles, Drysdale trained his weapon on Bryce. Slater kept his pointed at her.

When he finished, he tore off a final six-inch piece. He was planning to gag her, too. This was her final opportunity to scream for help.

But it wouldn't do any good. All her neighbors were too far away to hear. Except for possibly Matt and his father. And she couldn't expect help from either of them.

Besides, screaming would be a sure way for her to end up with a bullet in her head. Bryce, too.

Drysdale's gaze shifted to Bryce. "Tie them together, back-to-back. I don't want any chance of them escaping."

A cautious sense of relief filtered through her. If Drysdale was concerned about them escaping, he apparently didn't have plans to kill them. He just needed to secure them well enough that they couldn't call for help until he and his thugs were long gone. In fact, they probably had a private jet ready to take them to Grand Cayman or somewhere. Trying to scare her into selling the property didn't work, so maybe this was the backup plan.

Python pressed the short piece of tape over her mouth and brought her to a seated position. After jerking Bryce to his feet, he dragged him around the coffee table and shoved him to the floor behind her.

Once they were positioned back-to-back, Python circled their upper bodies three or four times with the tape.

Escape wouldn't be easy. Maybe some time would pass before they figured a way out of their predicament. If nothing else, eventually someone would check on them. Her aunt and uncle were expecting her tonight. If she didn't show up, they'd try to contact her. When that failed, they'd call the police.

"Slater, go get the gas."

Drysdale's words jarred her from her thoughts. *Gas?*

Dread wrapped around her, dark and thick and heavy. It bore down on her, pressing the air from her lungs. Her mind scrambled for an explanation, any explanation, all the while avoiding the obvious one.

When he returned a few minutes later, holding a gas can in one gloved hand, all denial fled.

Drysdale and his men planned to burn the house down with them inside.

Panic pounded up her spine and settled in her chest, sending her heart into a frenzied rhythm. At her back, Bryce twisted in a futile attempt to escape.

Slater started at the back door and sloshed gas along the wall, following the perimeter of the room. It splashed onto his jeans and shoes, and as he turned the corner and headed into the living room, he left wet footprints on the hardwood floor. After moving across the front and finishing the fourth wall, he splashed what was left in the can onto the couch.

Drysdale stood, staring down at her, shaking his head. "It wasn't supposed to come to this. I'm not a believer in the daughter paying for the sins of the father. But you brought it on yourself. Nothing happened until you refused to sell me the property. Almost nothing."

He glared at Python. "His instructions were to get up here and find the evidence. When he learned you were headed back up, he took it on himself to run you off the road. Had to drive his truck home and come back in Slater's vehicle, then thought I should have to pay for the damages."

Python crossed his massive arms. "How was I supposed to look for evidence if she was staying at the house? Running her off the road bought us time."

Andrea watched him, her final question now answered. He only thought it had bought them time. He hadn't counted on her getting off that slope and making it to the Murphy house less than two hours later.

Drysdale ignored the argument, his attention still on Andrea. "All you needed to do was sell. A few No Trespassing signs, and our secret would have been safe until we could locate what your father had taken, no matter how long it took."

He walked with Python to the back door. Slater followed, shoes still leaving wet tracks.

Shoes that looked familiar and she wasn't sure why. *Matt's shoes.*

That was where she'd seen them, sitting on Matt's front porch. The men were going to set the house on fire and leave Matt's gas-soaked shoes somewhere nearby.

That was why Drysdale hadn't shot them. He wanted to make sure none of the evidence led to him.

And all of it pointed to her antagonistic next-door neighbor.

The three men walked through the dining area and slipped out the back door. A minute later, Python stepped back inside and dropped a flaming stick on the floor.

The fire spread rapidly, following the path along the wall and licking at the curtains. Soon the entire double room would be engulfed in flames, with her and Bryce in the center.

God, please save us. Her biggest takeaway from the church services she'd attended the past two Sundays was that God was with her, not just at Christmas but all the time.

Please send someone.

He could do it. She had no doubt. She'd never questioned the greatness of God. She'd just believed in a distant God who didn't involve himself in the lives of people.

But the past two Sundays, she'd been introduced to a God who was much closer, a God who cared about every detail of her life—*God with us.*

She still believed in the greatness of God.

But if He chose not to answer, she only hoped that the smoke would take them out before the flames.

As flames traveled around the perimeter of the room, Bryce struggled against the tape holding him. Behind him, Andi screamed against hers, her cries little more than a muffled whimper. He'd never have let the man restrain him if the other hadn't been holding a pistol to her head. *God, help me get us out of here.*

He glanced frantically around him, pulse pounding in his ears. Tied as they were, they'd never get on their feet. Even if they could manage it and somehow hop to either door, they wouldn't be able to escape before the flames consumed them.

Their only hope was getting loose. Duct tape tore easily once the edge was ripped. He had a folding knife in his front pocket but no way to reach it.

His gaze settled on the coffee table. If he could tip the glass over and smash it with his boot, maybe they could use a piece of it to cut the tape. With the table at his right side, he'd have to turn ninety degrees to do what he had in mind. He rocked back and forth, pulling Andi with him, rotating a little with each movement. Andi likely had no idea what he planned to do, but she worked with him anyway.

A high-pitched whine sounded over the crackle of flames. His heart leaped. Sirens. Was help on its way?

No, that was impossible. The flames wouldn't be visible from outside for another couple of minutes. Then they'd spread fast. By the time someone called and emergency personnel arrived, it would be too late to save them. It was up to him.

He lifted his legs and tipped over the glass. When he brought his heels down hard, it shattered. Two curved sections, almost two square inches, lay among the smaller pieces.

Flames climbed up the back of the recliner, and smoke billowed above their heads. Bryce scooped the glass off the table and onto the floor. Now that Andi had figured out what he was doing, positioning them so he could reach it went much faster.

He picked up one of the larger pieces and slid it between her fingers. She immediately tightened her grip, holding it firm. He rubbed the edge of the tape against the glass.

Fire danced across the front of the room, moving up the gas-doused tree with a roar. He attacked the tape with renewed vigor. The piece of glass twisted, and pain went through his wrist, razor-sharp. Moisture trickled into his palm. Andi had lost her grip. She may have gotten cut, too.

Clasping his hands, he jerked his wrists outward. At the rip of tape, he heaved a relieved sigh. After a second tug, his hands were free. It took only a minute to slice through the tape that wrapped his ankles and bound the two of them together.

He removed it from their mouths, then worked on freeing her hands and ankles. Blood coated his palm and dripped from the ends of his fingers, making the glass slippery. His wrist was bleeding pretty badly. He'd deal with it once he'd gotten them both to safety.

A coughing spasm overtook him, and he pressed his jacket to his mouth. The whole perimeter of the room was engulfed in flames, the couch and curtains now on fire. They couldn't get to either door.

A wave of dizziness swept over him. Still on his hands and knees, he swayed sideways. The whole room was spinning. He blinked several times, trying to make it stop.

He had to get out. And he had to save Andi. He didn't know about her, but he wasn't ready to meet God. Two weeks ago, he would have thought he'd be welcomed through the pearly gates. Now he knew better.

"Come on." Andi took one of his hands and started to stand.

"Stay low. The smoke…"

The sirens seemed to be closer, somewhere out on the four-lane. Or maybe the squeal was inside his head.

Andi crawled toward the hall. "Follow me."

He forced his limbs to cooperate. Andi was ahead of him, casting repeated glances over her shoulder. He was moving through a tunnel, the walls closing in on him.

When they reached the master bedroom, she slammed the door behind him. Good thinking. It would buy them some time. He opened his mouth to say so but couldn't seem to formulate the words.

She threw open the front window. "Come on. We'll climb out through here."

He grasped the footboard and pulled himself onto the bed. She'd told him to do something, but he could no longer remember what.

She spun to face him. "Bryce?"

A second later, she'd closed the gap between them. When she looked at her hands, she gasped. "You're bleeding. You got cut when the glass slipped." She checked his wrist. "Lay down, and keep pressure on it. I need to find something I can use for a tourniquet."

She pushed him back onto the bed. Something slid from his pocket. She'd taken his phone. She stalked into the bathroom with it pressed to her ear. Her words drifted to him. "We need an ambulance and a fire truck." She rattled off the address.

The sirens grew closer. That had to be what he was hearing. His ears were ringing, but this was much louder, more piercing. Someone must have called before Andi did. Or the vehicles were responding to a different location.

Andi stepped into view, holding what used to be a

washcloth. It was now cut into strips. She also held…a toothbrush?

She tied one of the strips loosely around his forearm and slid the toothbrush underneath. As she turned it, the makeshift tourniquet tightened. The bleeding gradually stopped. Once satisfied, she tied another strip to secure everything in place.

There was a crash at the other end of the house. Maybe the roof had caved in. No, someone was there. There were shouts, raised men's voices.

Andi hurried to the open window and screamed for help. When Bryce pushed himself upright, the room spun and darkness moved in on the edges of his vision. Two figures appeared at the window.

"We need help." Andi's voice held panic. "Bryce has lost a lot of blood. I don't think he can make it out on his own."

Someone climbed through the window and dropped to the floor.

Matt?

No way was Matt risking his life to rescue them. Loss of blood was making him delirious.

But his rescuer *was* Matt. Andi looped one of his arms over her shoulders and Matt positioned himself under Bryce's other arm. Outside, the sirens reached ear-piercing level, then fell abruptly silent.

Andi and Matt brought him to his feet, and the darkness encroached further. As they lifted him into the window opening, strong hands outside gripped him around the torso and pulled him through. His rescuer tried to place him on his feet, but his knees buckled and his eyes drifted shut.

Someone dropped to the ground beside him and nestled a shoulder under his arm. That would be Matt. Was Andi still inside? He needed to help her.

But his legs wouldn't work. Matt and his other rescuer dragged him away from the house and laid him on the ground. Bryce forced his eyes open and looked up into the face of Jimmy Langman. Red and blue lights flashed around him.

"Andi…"

Soft hands wrapped around one of his. "I'm here."

She was safe, and so was he. Neither of them were going to meet God tonight. But the thought had shaken him. At the earliest opportunity, he was going to find out what it took to be ready and make sure he was.

Soon Andi's driveway held both an ambulance and a fire truck, in addition to the two sheriff cruisers that had arrived.

As the paramedics worked on him, bits and pieces of conversation drifted to him from nearby, questions from Andi that he couldn't make out, responses from Matt that made no sense—

"…the hospital…the old mine…buried…wearing my shoes…called the cops…fire…Bryce's truck…"

His eyes fell closed.

The words faded.

And everything went silent.

TWELVE

Andrea gave two raps on the doorjamb, then entered Bryce's hospital room.

He smiled from his bed, where he'd raised the back and propped a pillow behind him. "Hello, stranger."

"Hey." She returned his smile, her heart swelling. She loved him. After they'd both come so close to losing their lives, she could no longer deny it. Had last night's events had the same impact on him? If so, would he be willing to give a relationship a shot?

Would she?

His gaze slid over her. "Since you're dressed in street clothes rather than a hospital gown, I'm guessing they didn't keep you."

"They treated me for smoke inhalation, then released me this morning. I just finished all the discharge paperwork. Paige is picking me up when I'm ready to leave, but I figured I'd come up here and bug you first."

She'd gotten a hold of Tanner through the Murphy Police Department, and he'd given her Paige's number. She now had it programmed in her phone. She'd met her less than two weeks ago, but they'd instantly connected. Paige had lived through her own traumas.

Bryce nodded. "If you hold out a while longer, I might be able to join you. The doctor's releasing me today. I'll have to see him in ten days to have the stitches removed."

He held up one arm, with its thickly wrapped wrist. "He said as much blood as I lost, I was blessed to be alive. We nicked an artery." He grinned, shaking his head. "I can't believe you stopped the bleeding with a washcloth and toothbrush."

"Necessity is the mother of invention."

He took her hand with his good one and squeezed it. "I owe you my life."

"I owe you mine. If you hadn't broken the glass and cut the tape, we'd have died in the living room."

"And as unlikely as it seems, we might both owe our lives to Matt and his father."

"I prayed that God would send help, and He did, in the most unexpected way." She frowned. "But both of them made it clear they weren't doing it for us."

His brows drew together. "Then why?"

"Matt knew I was in the hospital, and you were spending all your time with me. He figured he'd take the opportunity to snoop around the old mine. While he was there, three men approached. He said he barely got himself hidden before they started poking around, talking about something being buried there, and once the Wheaton kid was out of the picture, they'd dig up the whole area if they had to."

"So why did he call the cops?"

"He didn't like them horning in on what he was doing. But what really did it was seeing the one guy wearing his shoes. He knew they were going to do something bad and make it look like he did it, the same as they'd done with the gas can and wrench. So he ran home and called the cops, not realizing we'd come back."

Bryce nodded. "So Matt didn't suddenly develop a Good Samaritan gene."

"'Fraid not. Anyway, a short time later, he slipped back over to see what was happening and saw Drysdale and his guys jogging away from the house. He started to follow them, hoping he'd be able to lead the police to them, then got scared and doubled back. That's when he realized the house was on fire and called 911 again."

"No wonder they got there so fast."

"Yeah. They were responding to Matt's calls, not mine. Matt didn't go around front until the police were almost there. That's when he saw your truck and realized we were inside. He ran home to get his dad. They kicked in the door, and I screamed for help. The rest you know."

Bryce pursed his lips. "Maybe they *were* watching out for their own interests, but we still owe them a huge debt of gratitude."

"I tried." She'd thought this could be the start of reconciliation between their families. But she wasn't holding out hope. There was as much animosity between them as there'd ever been. "They both said to keep my thanks. Langman said if we had died, Matt would have taken the blame and never seen the light of day, and that was the only reason they did what they did."

Bryce shrugged. "Maybe someday. You never know what the future has in store."

She nodded. The words were truer than he probably realized. She'd have never guessed when she showed up in Murphy last month, that in so short a time, she and Bryce would go from uneasy acquaintances to...

To what?

Bryce had dispelled the tension between them by laying it all out—he wasn't interested in anything deeper than friendship. At the time it had been a relief. That was when she'd been sure she'd wanted the same thing. And falling in love hadn't even been a dim possibility.

Should she do what he did, have a heart-to-heart talk and let him know exactly how she felt?

No. She'd already experienced the ultimate rejection once this year. If Bryce told her he didn't have those kinds of feelings for her, she'd want to go to bed and stay there.

Besides, if Bryce *was* interested in renewing a romantic relationship, she wasn't even sure she could go through with it. Maybe she would come to realize her walls were too thick, her heart too tattered to love again.

She pulled her hand from his grasp to slide a chair up to his bed. "Paige said as soon as you get out, we're all getting together at Tanner's for a party. She's calling it a celebration of life and justice."

Bryce lifted a brow. "Since we'll be celebrating justice, is it safe to assume Drysdale and his goons have been caught?"

"Yep. And police are going to be investigating everything Drysdale was involved in." She frowned, dread wrapping around her like a cloak. "I know it's not likely, but I keep hoping they'll uncover evidence that totally absolves my father."

His eyes filled with sadness. "That's sometimes hard to prove, piecing everything together after the fact. If they don't come to that conclusion, it doesn't mean your dad *was* involved, just that they can't eliminate the possibility."

"Thank you." She gave him a weak smile. She appreciated his words. But he wasn't just trying to make her feel better. He was probably trying to convince himself, too. Finding out her dad was innocent would be as important to him as it was her.

A man wearing a white jacket entered the room. A stethoscope dangled from his neck, and he held a clipboard. "Are you ready to get out of here?"

"More than you can imagine."

While the doctor gave Bryce instructions on the care of his wound, she stood back and waited.

Today was Friday. Next week, she'd be moving ahead with the purchase of Angie's business. Though she'd missed her appointment at the store, Angie had visited her in the hospital after her car wreck, and they'd had numerous phone conversations. Soon she wouldn't just be a Murphy resident. She'd be a Murphy business owner.

And she'd be living right next door to Bryce. So close, but never more than friends. Maybe quitting her job and moving to Murphy on a permanent basis had been a mistake.

She crossed her arms and leaned back against the wall. She'd made the choice abruptly, without thinking it through. Maybe it was time to give it a little more thought, before she proceeded down a track that couldn't be reversed. One she regretted.

Backing out of her purchase of Angie's business after giving her word would be a stinky thing to do. But it wasn't too late. Nothing had been signed, no money exchanged.

And she hadn't shut the door on her Atlanta job. She'd given notice but promised to be available remotely as long as needed. As dismayed as the company had been to lose her, they'd probably be pleased to bring her back on. If they hadn't already filled it, they'd likely even hire her for her old job.

Staying in Murphy or going back to Atlanta. Both choices had pros and cons.

Could she pray for wisdom? Was *God with us* just for comfort and protection? Or could it also apply to guidance?

She hoped so.

Because she was in serious need of some.

Bryce sat in Tanner's living room, surrounded by some of his favorite people. He'd been released from the hospital this afternoon. As promised, his friends had planned a celebration—a dinner of taco salad, complete with cake.

Colton and Mandy had brought meat and tortilla chips. Tanner had provided sour cream, salsa and cheese, and Paige had cut up lettuce and tomato. The four of them had gone in together on a cake from the Ingles bakery.

Since Bryce's friends had insisted that the party was in his and Andi's honor, they wouldn't let the two of them bring anything. Now he was sitting on the couch next to Andi, pleasantly full and sweet tooth satisfied.

Tanner stood to gather the empty cake plates and grinned at Bryce. "Since there are no more crazies stalking Andi, you're not going to know what to do with yourself."

Bryce smiled, too, a sense of lightness filling his chest. He'd caught them up on everything that had happened over the past few days. "Number one will be taking the obnoxious notification off my cell phone. I've been listening to Alvin and the Chipmunks on steroids for the past two weeks rather than risk missing another text from Andi."

"I'd be doing the same thing." Colton cast a loving glance at Mandy next to him. He'd been alternating between hugging eighteen-month-old Liam and bouncing him on one knee since they'd finished eating.

Mandy smiled and patted his leg.

A pang shot through Bryce. Seeing the happiness his friends had found shone a spotlight on his own loneliness.

Colton stood, holding his son against his chest. "We've had fun, but it's past this little guy's bedtime."

Andi pushed herself to her feet. "I think I'll head out, too. It's been a long day."

Bryce agreed. By the time they'd left the hospital, it had been early afternoon. Andi had asked Paige to drop her off so she could pick up another rental car and get checked into a motel. Then Paige had left him at the Wheaton place to get his Sorento. Fortunately, it was undamaged.

After hugs from the women and pats on the back from the men, Colton and his family loaded into their Highlander and Andi climbed into her vehicle, this time an Explorer. The two SUVs rolled up the drive, and Bryce made his way to his own.

Tanner followed him, but Paige disappeared inside. She lived in the cabin at the back of Tanner's property and wouldn't be joining Tanner in the house until after their wedding next April.

Tanner stopped next to his SUV. "Are you going to let her get away twice?"

Bryce looked at him, but his friend's attention was

on the Explorer, now making its turn onto 294. "What's that supposed to mean?"

"You know what I mean. You've kicked yourself the past twelve years for letting her get away the first time. Now you're getting a second chance. She's clearly in love with you. And you're going to blow it again."

He frowned at his friend rather than giving him the shove he wanted to. "Have you been talking to Colton?"

Tanner shrugged.

Yeah, just what he thought. His friends were conspiring against him.

Tanner gave him a nudge. "What are you afraid of?"

"Nothing." He'd given the answer on reflex. He'd answered too quickly, because what he'd said wasn't even true.

He *was* afraid. Afraid of rejection. Afraid she'd agree to pursue a relationship with him, then back off. Afraid now that he'd fallen head over heels in love with her, she'd go back to her ex-husband.

Tanner stared him down. "I don't believe you."

"Believe what you want." He opened the door to the Sorento and slid into the driver's seat. Before he could close the door, Tanner stepped into the opening.

He heaved a sigh. Colton and Tanner were the only two men on the planet who could push him like that.

"What do you want?"

Tanner leaned against the open door and rested a hand on the roof. "I want you to be happy, bro. So tell me why you're getting ready to make the biggest mistake of your life a second time."

He crossed his arms. "Okay, let's say she agrees to

date me. What do you think will happen if her ex real-
izes what he lost and wants her back?"

"From the little I know of Andi, I'd guess she'd tell
him to take a hike."

Bryce banged his head against the headrest a couple
of times. "I'm a cop. Her ex is a neurosurgeon. You think
there's any way I can compete with that?"

Tanner gave him a *get real* look. "The creep cheated
on her."

"And Pam's ex beat her up. Repeatedly. That didn't
stop her from dumping me and going back to him."

"I think Andi's got it together better than Pam did."

She did. But she was also practical. She'd been in
love with the guy once or she wouldn't have married
him. Sure, when she'd caught him with his girlfriend,
she'd been hurt. But she'd also been hurt all those years
ago when she'd stepped out of her woods and caught
him with Carla.

They were two entirely different situations. But it
didn't matter. If given the opportunity, restoring her
marriage would be the more practical choice.

Tanner looked ready to shake him. "You're not competing with anyone. You're the one she loves."

Bryce gave him a doubt-infused glance. "She told
you that."

"Not directly. But Paige commented on it. She had it
figured out the first time she met her. And it's as obvious on you as it is on Andi."

He sighed. "It doesn't matter. She's been burned. She's
got walls around her heart a mile thick. I don't have what
it takes to break them down."

"Then maybe you need to figure out what it does

take and work on getting it." He stepped back. "Think about it, bro."

Tanner shut the Sorento's door and raised a hand in farewell.

As Bryce headed up the drive to begin his short trip home, conflicting emotions tumbled through him. Tanner made it sound so easy. Of course, he'd found the girl of his dreams and was still flying high. Tanner and Paige were perfect together.

And so were he and Andi. They always had been. He'd seen it way back when they were teenagers. Then he'd lost sight of the fact.

He made a left at the four-lane and headed toward Ranger. Tanner was right. He *did* love her. And if he let her go again, he was going to regret it for the rest of his life. Whatever effort he had to expend, Andi was worth it.

Tanner had said he needed to figure it out. He had to somehow break down the walls she'd built around her heart.

Could they roll back time and return to the way they were?

No, they couldn't. They were different people. They couldn't have what they had before, a love that was pure and innocent. Maybe even a bit naive.

But that didn't mean they couldn't have something just as satisfying. Even more so. Something deeper. More meaningful because of everything they'd gone through to get there.

But first, Andi would have to be willing to take a chance on him. The only way he was going to get past her defenses was to convince her that he really did love her the way he'd said he did all those years ago. With a love as big as the sky. Always and forever.

Whatever he did, it would have to be something special. Mere words wouldn't do it. Neither would gifts.

A plan began to form. By the time he pulled into his driveway, it was taking shape. He wouldn't be able to pull it off alone. He'd need help.

A partner in crime.

And he knew just the person.

THIRTEEN

Andrea stood back, watching people enter the large room, gazes filled with appreciation. With its wooden floors, brick walls and open-beam ceiling, the Hackney Warehouse was rich with character and a popular venue for weddings and other events. This one was an engagement party, the first job Andrea had done without Angie's assistance.

She'd moved ahead with purchasing the business and, in the three weeks since Christmas, had accompanied Angie on four decorating jobs. She couldn't say God had spoken to her. But He'd given her peace about the decision. Wasn't that sort of the same thing?

She'd also gained peace about something else. She wasn't sure whether to credit God with it, but she was thanking Him anyway. The investigation was progressing well. Drysdale and his cronies had tried hard to implicate her father, but they hadn't been able to totally cover their tracks. Her father's assets were still frozen, pending the final results of the investigation, but what had been uncovered so far was encouraging.

Her father's partners had had quite a thing going. Drysdale had been acquiring bogus geological reports

showing rich mineral deposits, and Lassiter and Barrand had been presenting the information to investors.
They'd brought her father in a year and a half earlier.
Judging from the changes she'd noticed in him, he'd discovered something was off about nine months before he
died. With so much evidence pointing to him, that might
have been why he'd wanted to get some direction from
Bryce first.

A woman approached, wearing a rust-colored sweater
dress with a wide black belt and fur-topped black boots.
"Everything's absolutely perfect. Everyone's gushing
about the decorations." Blond curls bounced as she ges-
tured.

Andrea gave her an appreciative smile. Shelby Pe-
ters was her client. She radiated excitement, and Andrea
had to tamp down some unexpected jealousy. If she was
going to envy all her brides-to-be, she'd gotten into the
wrong line of work.

She cast a glance around the room to take in the decorations that everyone was "gushing" about. Tulle-covered
strands of lights wound around the columns, and swags
of tulle and lights hung from the ceiling. Long rows of
tables were draped in white linen, with centerpieces of
tulle, flowers, greenery and candles every few feet.

A DJ had set up in the corner and was already provid-
ing music for the attendees. Soon one hundred and fifty
guests would sit down to a full catered dinner. Shelby
and the groom-to-be had obviously spared no expense.

She brought her attention back to her client. "So where
is the handsome guy?" All her dealings had been with
Shelby, and she had yet to meet the groom.

"He should be here shortly."

When Bryce walked into the room, Andrea's pulse

picked up speed and her stomach rolled over. Dressed to a tee in a suit and tie, he looked better than good. She needed to stop reacting to him, no matter what he was wearing.

Since the fire, she'd been living in town, so with the exception of church and a couple of gatherings with Bryce's friends, she hadn't seen much of him.

She should have known she'd be likely to run into him tonight. He knew everybody. If Shelby or her fiancé had been Murphy residents for any length of time, he'd be a friend of at least one of them.

He walked toward her, his warm smile making her weak in the knees. She silently scolded herself. Even if he *was* interested in a romantic relationship, it would never work. If she couldn't hold on to him back then, what made her think she could hold on to him now? Or that she had what it took to keep any man's love? She hadn't been able to make her relationship with Phil last. Even with a marriage license.

When Bryce reached her, he was still smiling. It was more disarming up close.

"You outdid yourself. Everything looks great."

"Thank you." She was pleased with the effect. And she'd thoroughly enjoyed the process. Any doubts she'd had about whether she'd made the right decision had dissipated with her first job. The creativity that she'd been so sure was too deeply buried to resurrect had come charging to the surface like a geyser.

Bryce looked around the room. "Isn't Paige here? She'd said she was working with you."

"She went to the ladies' room."

The employee that usually helped with decorating jobs had gotten sick, but Paige was able to clear her

schedule and step in last minute. Shelby had insisted
that they both stay and enjoy the festivities. That wasn't
typical. Usually, she'd clear out before the first guests
arrived and come back when the event was over to tear
down.

"So, are you a friend of the bride or the groom?"

"I know them both really well."

More guests arrived, and Andrea recognized several
familiar faces. Tanner was on the guest list, as were
Colton and Mandy. They'd apparently left Liam with a
babysitter.

Soon the DJ stopped the music to tell everyone to take
a seat. When Paige and Tanner sat on one side of her, and
Mandy and Colton sat on the other, she tamped down
disappointment. Bryce had taken a seat at the opposite
end of another row rather than sitting with her. And why
not? She wasn't the only friend he had.

The DJ cleared the guests to go through the buffet
line, one long table at a time. Soon everyone had their
food, and the hum of conversation rose against a background of love songs.

She'd just finished eating when the DJ stopped the
music and called Bryce up. He hurried forward and
grabbed the microphone.

"Is everyone having a good time?" Applause rose
around her. "How's the food?" More applause, even
louder.

What was Bryce doing up there? Was he the best man,
ready to toast the groom-to-be? Had the man even arrived? If he had, Shelby hadn't introduced him.

"I want to start by asking a very special lady to join
me up here."

Andrea nodded. That would be Shelby. They were apparently close.

"Andi Wheaton."

Her stomach rolled over and dropped several inches. She swiveled her head between Paige and Mandy. "Me?"

They both smiled. "Yes, you."

When she sat in stupefied silence, Paige gave her a little push. "Go."

Andrea rose from her chair and made her way to the front corner of the room. What was he doing?

She released a breath. He was going to recognize her for the decorations. Next he'd recognize the caterers.

When she reached him, he turned her to face the crowd and looped an arm over her shoulders, his other hand still holding the mic. "This is Andi Wheaton. Her business is Designs by Andi, formerly Designs by Angie. She's responsible for the decorations tonight."

The room filled with applause and whistles. Heat crept up her neck and into her cheeks. But Bryce was giving her free publicity. She'd take it.

When the applause died down, he dropped his arm from her shoulders and took her hand. "I first met Andi when we were about six and she and her dad came to visit. By age twelve, I started to realize girls were pretty cool and Andi was especially intriguing."

Some chuckles went around the room. Her cheeks were now on fire. What was Bryce doing? This wasn't about them. It was Shelby's party.

But Bryce continued. "By age fourteen, I was hopelessly in love. At least as in love as one can be at that age." Some more chuckles. "At age fifteen, I realized she was in love with me, too, and we shared our first kiss."

Andrea closed her eyes. *Oh, God, please open a hole*

in the floor and let me disappear. She was so going to kill Bryce when this was over.

She opened her eyes and sought out Shelby, who was sitting in the front row, next to a young man Andi was sure had to be her fiancé. He'd apparently slipped in after they'd gotten up to fill their plates.

If Shelby had a problem with Bryce horning in on her special night, she didn't show it. In fact, she wore a radiant smile.

Bryce continued, his tone somber. "When I turned eighteen, I lost her."

The room fell totally silent, so quiet there wasn't even a cough or rustle of clothing. Andrea clenched her teeth. She needed to put a stop to this before Bryce embarrassed her, or himself, any further.

"This is Shelby's party." She hissed the words, hoping they'd reach his ears but not the microphone. "Anything you have to say to me can wait."

Bryce ignored her. "Shelby, can you please come up here?"

If she couldn't stop him, maybe Shelby could. Maybe she'd throw him out. Maybe she'd throw them both out.

But she didn't look like someone ready to expel guests from her party. When she stepped up beside them, she was smiling even more broadly. Bryce's smile matched his friend's.

"Andi, meet my cousin, Shelby. My *married* cousin." He lifted her left hand, where both an engagement and wedding band circled her ring finger.

"But—" She looked from Shelby's hand to her face, then back to Bryce, feeling like the only one not in on some practical joke. "If Shelby's already married, why are we here?"

Shelby gave her an apologetic smile. But there was too much joy behind it for the apology to look sincere. "Sorry. I'm afraid I got you here under false pretenses." After a playful wave, she walked back to her seat.

Andrea might have followed, but her brain was too stalled out for her to do more than stand dumbstruck. Bryce turned her toward him and took both of her hands in his. Instead of speaking to her, he angled his face to the crowd.

"I'm going to do something now that is more than ten years past due."

He dropped to one knee, still holding her hands. Now his eyes were on her and no one else. Her mind spun. Actually, everything else inside seemed to be spinning, too.

"Andrea Wheaton, I love you with all my heart. Will you do me the honor of marrying me?"

Her jaw sagged. "You're proposing here?"

He released one of her hands to sweep his arm wide, indicating all those looking on, the caterers standing against the wall behind the long buffet table, the decorations.

"This engagement party is yours. If you'll say yes."

The pieces tried to fall into place, but she was still having a hard time wrapping her mind around everything. Bryce had planned all this. The whole thing had been his idea. Not only had he spent a fortune on the elaborate party, he was risking humiliation in front of all his friends if she said no. He had to be seriously in love with her.

But what if it didn't last? What if someone better came along? Going through that kind of rejection again would destroy her.

He squeezed her hands, doubt creeping across his features. She'd waited too long. But how could she make a decision like that spur of the moment? Would she ever be ready to let down her guard?

He continued to stare up at her, emotion swimming in his golden-brown eyes. Had his gaze ever held that much love? Had Phil's? She didn't think so.

"You love me?" Her words were the merest whisper.

"More than you can imagine."

"Always and forever?"

"Always and forever."

She looked around the room. Bryce had proved his love for her in a dramatic way. How could she still question his commitment?

She couldn't.

She gave his hands a tug, a silent command to rise. When he was on his feet, she pulled her hands from his grasp. Uncertainty flashed in his eyes for only a moment, turning to relief, then pure joy, when she slid her arms around his neck. His encircled her waist.

"Yes." She turned her head toward the crowd and spoke more loudly. "Yes."

Once again, applause rang out, but this time it didn't die down for some time.

The first strains of "Always and Forever" filled the room, and the overhead lights went out, leaving only the strands of tiny white lights that she'd used in her decorating.

As Luther Vandross crooned the words in his smooth, rich voice, Bryce began swaying to the music, and she fell into step with him.

He bent at the waist, mouth close to her ear. "Do you love me?"

"Yes."

"I want to hear you say it."

"I love you. I've been falling back in love with you bit by bit ever since I returned to Murphy. I think it started when I walked into your house and saw that you had my sketches proudly displayed. By the time you helped me set up the tree, and we were sitting side by side on the couch, a fire in the fireplace, I was hopeless."

"But you didn't let me kiss you."

"Because I was scared. I was scared of everything I was feeling for you and scared of being hurt."

He leaned close, his face inches from hers. "I don't want you to ever be afraid again."

No, she wouldn't. How could any doubts take up residence in her mind when he looked at her like that, as if she were the only thing in his life that he truly cherished?

He leaned closer still. He was going to kiss her, but this time she was ready.

His lips met hers. The awkwardness she should have felt knowing they had one hundred and fifty sets of eyes on them lasted all of three seconds. The DJ standing a few feet away, the party guests, the rows of tables—everything around her faded. It was just the two of them, her and this man she'd loved and then lost and then found again.

Warmth flowed through her, the sense of having come home. This was where she belonged. Right here in Murphy. In Bryce's arms.

When he pulled away, she almost protested. Her eyes met his, and the same adoration she'd seen earlier was shining from his face.

"You know when *I* started to love *you* again?"

"When?"

"I don't think I ever stopped."

He twirled her around and drew her closer. Her heart soared with the music.

Bryce loved her, and she loved him.
Always and forever.
With a love as big as the sky.

* * * * *

If you enjoyed this exciting story of
suspense and intrigue, pick up these other stories
from Carol J. Post:

Shattered Haven
Hidden Identity
Mistletoe Justice
Buried Memories
Reunited by Danger
Fatal Recall

Available now from Love Inspired Suspense!

Find more great reads at www.LoveInspired.com

Dear Reader,

I hope you've enjoyed returning to Murphy, North Carolina. A number of years ago, while visiting the area, my husband and I went in with four other family members and bought a dilapidated old cabin on twelve acres. While at the building supply store, we told them about our project, and the guy asked if we knew about the gold. We talked to some people, one of whom was a retired geologist who lived across the street at the time. Sure enough, turns out thar's gold in them thar hills! We found where mining had happened at one end of the property and also on the geologist's land. There's still gold, but it's about one thousand feet down, buried in a vein of quartz.

I hope you've enjoyed Bryce and Andrea's story. I love reunion stories, and this one was a lot of fun to write. Both Andrea and Bryce had acquired a lot of baggage over the years and had to work hard to learn to trust again.

I hope you'll come back in December to reconnect with some of your favorite Murphy residents in the third and final book in the series.

Love in Christ,
Carol J. Post

COMING NEXT MONTH FROM
Love Inspired® Suspense

Available October 2, 2018

BATTLE TESTED
Military K-9 Unit • by Laura Scott

Former air force pilot Isaac Goddard's only goal is to bring his late friend's dog home from combat—until he stumbles across an attack on nurse Vanessa Gomez. With the Red Rose Killer determined to make Vanessa his next victim, Isaac vows to guard her at all costs.

UNDERCOVER MEMORIES
by Lenora Worth

After waking up in the hospital, private investigator Emma Langston knows she was sent on an urgent case—but she can't remember her mission. Now someone wants her dead, and her only chance of surviving long enough to recover her memories is by relying on Detective Ryder Palladin for protection.

AMISH CHRISTMAS SECRETS
Amish Protectors • by Debby Giusti

When a man shows up at the nursing home where Amish single mother Rosie Glick works, demanding incriminating evidence her murdered boyfriend stole, Ezra Stoltz comes to her rescue. But with the killer dead set on silencing Rosie, Ezra must hide her and her baby to keep them safe.

IN TOO DEEP
by Sharon Dunn

After one of the at-risk teens she mentors calls her for help, Sierra Monforton witnesses a drug deal and becomes a target. And while undercover DEA agent Joseph Anderson's assignment is to take down a drug ring, he'll risk everything—including blowing his cover—to ensure Sierra doesn't get hurt.

GRAVE PERIL
by Mary Alford

Jamie Hendricks always believed her late father was innocent of murder... and now her uncle claims to have proof. Only CIA agent Gavin Dalton—her ex-boyfriend and the son of her father's supposed victim—can help her uncover a deadly conspiracy that goes deeper than anyone expected.

FRAMED FOR CHRISTMAS
by Jaycee Bullard

Someone's framing DNA technician Dani Jones for drug smuggling— and they plan to kill her to cover the truth. Can former DEA agent Gideon Marshall and his retired drug-sniffing dog make sure she survives long enough to find out why...and clear her name?

LISCNM0918

Get 4 FREE REWARDS!

We'll send you 2 FREE Books plus 2 FREE Mystery Gifts.

Love Inspired® Suspense books feature Christian characters facing challenges to their faith... and lives.

FREE Value Over **$20**

Looking for inspiration in tales
of hope, faith and heartfelt romance?

Check out **Love Inspired**® and
Love Inspired® **Suspense** books!

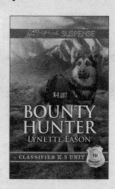

New books available every month!

CONNECT WITH US AT:

Harlequin.com/Community

 Facebook.com/HarlequinBooks

Twitter.com/HarlequinBooks

Instagram.com/HarlequinBooks

Pinterest.com/HarlequinBooks

ReaderService.com

Love Inspired®